# Verse and Worse

Also by Arnold Silcock

*

INTRODUCTION TO CHINESE ART AND HISTORY

# VERSE AND WORSE

★

A Private Collection

by

ARNOLD SILCOCK

with drawings by

V. H. DRUMMOND

FABER AND FABER
London

First published in 1952
by Faber and Faber Limited
3 Queen Square London WC1
First published in this edition 1958
Reprinted 1959, 1960, 1962, 1963, 1967, 1969 and 1971
Printed in Great Britain by
Latimer Trend & Co Ltd Whitstable
All rights reserved


ISBN 0 571 05132 4  *(Faber Paper Covered Edition)*

ISBN 0 571 04384 4  *(Hard Bound Edition)*

# Author-Editor's Dedication

To Those who Gave me Most I Give my Thanks;
You Helped me Make this Book.—Oh, Generous Ranks:
My Friends and Family!—Here Find your Roll
Of Names—in Order Alphabetical! . . .

*Mr. Peter W. Adams, Miss Winifred Ambler,
Mr. Robert Atkinson, Mr. Lewis Brace, Mr. Reginald Brundrit,
Mrs. Ernest Eyres & Mr. Laurence Eyres, Monsieur Albert Gervais, Mr. Edward I. Halliday, Sir Meyrick Hewlett, K.C.M.G.,
Lieut.-Colonel A. S. R. Hughes & Mrs. Sylvia Hughes, Dame
Laura Knight & Mr. Harold Knight, Mr. Arthur E. Lane, the
Rev. Dr. Nathaniel Micklem & Mrs. Agatha Micklem and Messrs.
Nathaniel, Robert & Ambrose Micklem, Miss Bridget Muller,
Miss Vivienne Mylne, 'Jane Oliver' (Mrs. John Llewelyn Rhys),
Mr. John Parr, Miss Gladys A. Peebles, Miss Monica Penn (Mrs.
Geoffrey Sheen-Carter) & Brigadier B. H. Penn, D.S.O., Mr.
Leslie Pott & Mrs. Norma Pott, Mr. Edgar Ranger & Mrs. Dora
Ranger, Mr. Arthur E. Shepherd, the Hon. Andrew Shirley, Miss
Diana Silcock (Mrs. Brian H. Christie), Miss Ruth Silcock, 'Ann
Stafford' (Mrs. Anne Pedler), Mr. Charles Sutro & Mrs. Evelyn
Sutro, Squadron-Leader Arthur R. Thomson, M.C., Mynheer
Arie Vandermeyden & Mevrow Alice Vandermeyden, Mr. G.
Grey Wornum.*

# Introduction, Foreword, Acknowledgments

Reader, there is no introduction to this book,
  But if for information you've a mind
  You'll find the foreword's got stuck in behind
(Unless you're too darned indolent to look.)

# Preface

Herein, Reader, are rhymes with ideas and origins as diverse and remote from each other as the Archbishop of Canterbury from the *Moulin Rouge*.

Among them is one, in fact, written in the sixteenth century by a former Bishop of Bath and Wells. His ludicrously apt name, redolent of cool cobwebby wine-cellars, sanded bars, dairy-maids and cheese, was Bishop Still: his subject—*Jolly Goode Ale and Olde!*

But—Come within for further refreshment. There are no closing hours here!

# Contents

# Good Old Guzzling and Drinking Days

★ ★ ★ ★ ★ ★ ★ ★ ★ ★ ★ ★ ★ ★ ★ ★ ★ ★ ★ ★ ★

*Good Health to you, Happy Reveller!*
*Here you will find an unconventional salad of good things (mixed*
à l'Américaine) *as pungent as cheese, as fresh as lettuce, as crisp*
*as endive, as tart as grapefruit, as sweet as sun-drenched raisins, as*
*smooth and mellifluous as exotic avocado, and as subtle as chicory.*
*And some, no doubt (the rude reader may add) ruddier than the ulti-*
*mate cherry!*

> Then as to feasting, it doesn't agree with me—
> Each single Goblet is equal to three with me,
> Wine is my foe, tho' I still am a friend of it,
> Hock becomes hic—with a cup at the end of it!
>
> OLIVER WENDELL HOLMES

> For if my pure libations exceed three,
> I feel my heart becomes so sympathetic,
> That I must have recourse to black *Bohee*;
> 'Tis pity wine should be so deleterious,
> For tea and coffee leave us much more serious.
>
> LORD BYRON

> I think that some have died of drought,
>     And some have died of drinking;
> I think that naught is worth a thought——
>     And I'm a fool for thinking!
>
> WINTHROP MACKWORTH PRAED: 1802–39

[15]

## THE IRISH PIG

'Twas an evening in November,
As I very well remember,
I was strolling down the street in drunken pride,
But my knees were all a'flutter
So I landed in the gutter,
And a pig came up and lay down by my side.

Yes, I lay there in the gutter
Thinking thoughts I could not utter,
When a colleen passing by did softly say,
'Ye can tell a man that boozes
By the company he chooses.'—
At that, the pig got up and walked away!

ANON: FROM DUBLIN: ORALLY COLLECTED

Lines from
BEER

O Beer! O Hodgson, Guiness, Allsopp, Bass!
 Names that should be on every infant's tongue!
Shall days and months and years and centuries pass,
 And still your merits be unrecked, unsung?
Oh! I have gazed into my foaming glass,
 And wished that lyre could yet again be strung
Which once rang prophet-like through Greece, and
  taught her
Misguided sons that the best drink was water. . . .


Oh! when the green slopes of Arcadia burned
 With all the lustre of the dying day,
And on Cithaeron's brow the reaper turned,
 (Humming, of course, in his delightful way,
How Lycidas was dead, and how concerned
 The Nymphs were when they saw his lifeless clay;
And how rock told to rock the dreadful story
That poor young Lycidas was gone to glory:)


What would that lone and labouring soul have given,
 At that soft moment for a pewter pot!
How had the mists that dimmed his eye been riven,
 And Lycidas and sorrow all forgot!
If his own grandmother had died unshriven,
 In two short seconds he'd have recked it not;
Such power hath Beer. The heart which Grief hath
  canker'd
Hath one unfailing remedy—the Tankard. . . .

[17]

But hark! a sound is stealing on my ear——
    A soft and silvery sound—I know it well.
Its tinkling tells me that a time is near
    Precious to me—it is the Dinner Bell.
O blessed Bell! Thou bringest beef and beer,
    Thou bringest good things more than tongue may
        tell:
Seared is, of course, my heart—but unsubdued
Is, and shall be, my appetite for food. . . .

                     C. S. CALVERLEY: 1831–84

## ON HERESY AND BEER

*Buttes, in 'Dyets Dry Dinner' (1599), gives the following:*
    Heresie and beere came hopping into
        England both in a yeere.

*But a correspondent in 'Notes and Queries' (1852) quotes another
version:*

        Hops, reformation, baize and beer,
        Came into England all in a year.

## FROM 'THE MIRROR' MAGAZINE OF
## 8 MARCH 1828:

*At a large party, at which Lady Erskine and Sheridan were
present, Lord Erskine declared that "a wife is only a tin canister tied
to one's tail". Next day Sheridan sent Lady Erskine the following
verses.*

    Lord Erskine at Woman presuming to rail
    Calls a wife 'a tin canister tied to one's tail',
    And fair Lady Anne, while the subject he carries on,
    Seems hurt at his lordship's degrading comparison.

But wherefore degrading? Considered aright,
A canister's polished and useful and bright;
And should dirt its original purity hide,
That's the fault of the puppy to whom it is tied.

*The same Richard Brinsley Sheridan wrote, in 'The Critic':*

> A bumper of good liquor
> Will end a contest quicker
> Than justice, judge, or vicar.


## HODGE'S GRACE

Heavenly Father bless us,
And keep us all alive;
There's ten of us for dinner
And not enough for five.

ANON


## A SCOTTISH GRACE

Oh Lord, who blessed the loaves and fishes,
Look doon upon these twa bit dishes,
And though the taties be but sma',
Lord, mak 'em plenty for us a';
But if our stomachs they do fill,
'Twill be anither miracle.

TRADITIONAL

## MANNERS

I eat my peas with honey
I've done it all my life
It makes the peas taste funny
But it keeps 'em on the knife!

ANON

## ON CHINA BLUE

On china blue my lobster red
Precedes my cutlet brown,
With which my salad green is sped
By yellow Chablis down.

Lord, if good living be no sin,
But innocent delight,
O polarize these hues within
To one eupeptic white.

SIR STEPHEN GASELEE

*By kind permission of the Wine and Food Society
and the President, Monsieur André L. Simon.*

## ODE TO A SALMON

Oh! for the thrill of a Highland stream,
With the bending rod of a fisherman's dream,
The screaming reel and flying line,
Where the far-flung pearl-drops wetly shine——
The sudden leap, then the silent strife,
While the salmon grimly fights for life;
As a worthy foe, or a regal dish,
We respect this gallant fighting fish.

But civilized man's besetting sin,
Is bunging food in a box or tin.
So into a tin that salmon goes,
Like Heinz Baked Beans, or Sturgeon Roes!
Those tidy tins travel far and wide,
With a so-called salmon tucked inside,
And they're sent as an airman's dainty feast
By devious routes to the Middle East!

That fish proceeds to haunt the men,
Who harried his life in the Highland glen;
He appears disguised as a round fishcake,
For breakfast; swiftly in its wake,

At lunch, in breadcrumbs fried in lard,
Built by the mile—cut off by the yard!
Then to the diner's outraged gaze,
Greasily swimming in mayonnaise!

Dressed in batter or bathed in sauces,
Clothed in parsley for other courses!——
To add one more to this fearful host,
The spectre appears—on cast-iron toast!
And in course of time, the remains we'll see
Dished up as salmon paste, for tea!

When at long last we live in peace,
The tin-opener's arduous task shall cease,
And we'll tell the Supply Branch for their sins,
Just what to do with their blood-red tins!
For, both in a river, and on a dish,
I hate that ubiquitous blasted fish.

> *Written by a Commander R.N., in col-*
> *laboration with a Pilot Officer, R.A.F.,*
> *and supplied by the last-named*—Flt.-
> Lieut. James McGregor, R.A.F.
> (*Edited*)

Lines from
## RECIPE FOR SALAD

Serenely full, the Epicure would say:
'Fate cannot harm me: I have dined to-day.'

SYDNEY SMITH

## POOR BEASTS!

The horse and mule live 30 years
And nothing know of wines and beers.
The goat and sheep at 20 die
And never taste of Scotch or Rye.
The cow drinks water by the ton
And at 18 is mostly done.
The dog at 15 cashes in
Without the aid of rum and gin.
The cat in milk and water soaks
And then in 12 short years it croaks.
The modest, sober, bone-dry hen
Lays eggs for nogs, then dies at 10.
All animals are strictly dry:
They sinless live and swiftly die;
But sinful, ginful, rum-soaked men
Survive for three score years and ten.
And some of them, a very few,
Stay pickled till they're 92.'

ANON

## 'WARE TOMATO-JUICE

An accident happened to my brother Jim
When somebody threw a tomato at him——
Tomatoes are juicy and don't hurt the skin,
But this one was specially packed in a tin.

ANON

Lines from
## JOLLY GOOD ALE & OLDE

I cannot eate but littyl meate,
My stomach is not goode
But sure I thinke that I can drinke
With him that wears a hood.
Though I go bare, take ye no care,
I nothing am a-cold;
I stuff my skin so full within
Of jolly goode ale and olde.
Back and side go bare, go bare
Both foot and hand go cold;
But, belly, God send thee goode ale enough,
Whether it be new or olde.

JOHN STILL
(BISHOP OF BATH AND WELLS: 1543–1608)

## AN OLD RHYME
INSCRIBED ON THE INN-SIGN OF 'THE PLOUGH'
AT FORD IN THE COTSWOLDS

Ye weary travelers that pass by,
With dust and scorching sunbeams dry,
Or be benumb'd with snow and frost,
With having these bleak cotswolds crosst,
Step in and quaff my nut-brown ale
Bright as rubys mild and stale.
'Twill make your laging trotters dance
As nimble as the suns of france.
Then ye will own, ye men of sense,
That neare was better spent six pence.

[24]

## A RHYME

### INSCRIBED ON THE INN-SIGN OF 'THE BEEHIVE' AT ABINGDON IN BERKSHIRE

Within this hive,
We're all alive,
Good liquor makes us funny,
So if you're dry,
Come in and try
The Flavour of our honey.

## A RHYME

### INSCRIBED ON A PINT POT

There are several reasons for drinking,
And one has just entered my head;
If a man cannot drink when he's living
How the Hell can he drink when he's dead?

ANON

## ALL THINGS HAVE SAVOUR

All things have savour, though some very small,
Nay, a box on the eare hath no smell at all.

OLD SAYING

## EPITAPH ON A DRUNKARD

He had his beer
From yeare to yeare
And then his bier had him.

ANON

## A MITEY SAMSON

Jack, eating rotten cheese, did say,
Like Samson I my thousands slay:
I vow, quoth Roger, so you do.
And with the self-same weapon too!

BENJAMIN FRANKLIN

## THE PALACE

### LINES FROM THE POEM ON A GUILD 'OUTING' AT THE OLD CRYSTAL PALACE

To catch the destin'd train—to pay
   Their willing fares, and plunge within it——
Is, as in old Romaunt they say,
   With them the work of half-a-minute.
Then off they're whirl'd, with songs and shouting,
To cedared Sydenham for their outing.

Kerchief in hand I saw them stand
   In every kerchief lurk'd a lunch;
When they unfurl'd them, it was grand
   To watch bronzed men and maidens crunch
The sounding celery-stick, or ram
The knife into the blushing ham.

Dash'd the bold fork through pies of pork;
   O'er hard-boil'd eggs the saltspoon shook;
Leapt from its lair the playful cork:
   Yet some there were, to whom the brook
Seem'd sweetest beverage, and for meat
They chose the red root of the beet.

[26]

But ah! what bard could sing how hard,
  The artless banquet o'er, they ran
Down the soft slope with daisies starr'd
  And kingcups! onward, maid with man,
They flew, to scale the breezy swing,
Or court frank kisses in the ring.

Such are the sylvan scenes that thrill
  This heart! The lawns, the happy shade,
Where matrons, whom the sunbeams grill,
  Stir with slow spoon their lemonade;
And maidens flirt (no extra charge)
In comfort at the fountain's marge! . . .

C. S. CALVERLEY

# Accent on Accent: The Accident of Ancestry

★ ★ ★ ★ ★ ★ ★ ★ ★ ★ ★ ★ ★ ★ ★ ★ ★ ★ ★ ★ ★ ★ ★ ★

*Almost the funniest, yet almost the least well known of the forms of broken English is the brand spoken in the old Treaty-ports of China. 'Pidgin-English' originally meant 'Business English' for the word 'pidgin' itself was the nearest the average Chinese could get to a pronunciation of the word 'business'. So 'pidgin' now means business and affair or matter or way of life or method—unless birds are in the wind, when 'pidgin', at last, means 'pigeon'! Consequently 'love-pidgin' means making love, 'joss-pidgin' is religion, and 'look-see-pidgin' is hypocrisy. But 'pidgin-eye' means a pigeon's eye or good sight!*

*Enunciation of the consonant R is another impossible feat for most Chinese, and their attempts result in a sound resembling L. Therefore in the following verses L, in italics, represents the letter R. The commonest examples are, velly for very: cly-cly for cry: plopa for proper: solly for sorry: flin for friend.*

*Other common variations on English words are, chilo for child: allo for all: alloway for always: in fact the Chinese love to add an 'o' whenever possible, and a fool is foolo, while others as easily recognizable are, debilo for devil: golo for gold: waifo for wife.*

*The Chinese are also especially fond of adding an 'ee' sound to any word at will—like 'squeezey' for squeeze: 'tinkee' for think: 'supposey' for suppose: 'blongey' for belong.*

*As in the Chinese language itself Pidgin-English makes no distinction between* he, she, it *and* they, *and* his, hers, its, *and* theirs, *so* 'he' *is commonly used to denote any of these words.* 'My' *is indiscriminately used for* I, me, my, mine, we, our *and* ours!

*Finally* 'maskee' *is a very common word meaning* 'however', *or* 'without', *or* 'no matter', *or* 'also', *or* 'anyhow', *or* 'but', *or* 'in spite of'! *While* 'galow' *means absolutely nothing, and is even more common!*

*A good test for any exasperated reader is the following snippet from Leland's story of the cat who was converted and wore a rosary.*

> One time lib China-side one piecee cat,
> One day he massa take Joss-pidgin beads
> He put bead *l*ound cat neck.

*But the conversion, though apparent to the mice, was not real:*

> Wat-time he mousey walk outside he hole,
> Look-see dat pidgin—see dat cat hab catch
> One piecee bead, he mousey too much glad.

*They gather round and celebrate the conversion of* 'one-piecee cat', *in these words:*

> ... 'One tim he ve*ll*y bad—but now he 'pent
> An' nevva chow-chow mousey any more,
> An allo mousey lib all *pl*opa now;
> He go outside what-tim he wantchee go,
> An' nevva blongey *fl*aid—he cat no fear.
> An' mousey go to sing-song allo tim,
> An' takee waifo, chilos walk outside,
> An' allo day for allo mousey now,
> He be one Feast ob Lantern, *hai! ch'hoy!*'
> T'at mousey tink t'at pidgin ve*ll*y nice,

He catchee too much happy iniside,
He makee dancee, galantee, maskee.

*But one string of beads is not a sufficiently powerful Joss to turn
one piecee velly bad cat into one Joss-pidgin cat; and he creeps, man-
man (slowly) towards the joyous mouse party.*

He cat look-see t'at dance, he walk man-man,
No makee bobbely till wat-tim he come
Long-side he dancee—t'en he lun chop-chop
Insidee dance and catch one piecee mouse,
An' makee chow-chow all same olo tim.

*And the dead mouse's friends all run away and hide.*

He mousey flin all wailo in he hole,
An' allo cly-cly—some for he dead flin,
An' some what fo' he flaid cat catchee he;
An' allo-tim t'ey makee one sing-song,
Sing-song how mousey solly iniside. . . .

*This one little rhyme contains most of the usual phrases and forms
peculiar to Pidgin-English. For instance 'wat-tim' for what time or
when: 'galantee' for gallant in the sense of gay and grand: 'bobbely'
for a commotion: 'man-man' for slowly (a word 'lifted' direct from
the Chinese) and 'chop-chop' meaning quickly.*

*It was Charles Godfrey Leland, an American poet, and author of
the famous 'Hans Breitmann Ballads', so full of humour and pathos,
who also was the only poet to write verse in and popularize Pidgin-
English. Born in Philadelphia in 1824 he studied at the Universities
of Princeton, Heidelberg, Munich, and Paris, and was in the Paris
Revolution of 1848. He became a barrister, a journalist and author,
and a much travelled and versatile worker and writer in the fields of
education and handicrafts (especially wood-carving, on which he*

*wrote two or three books), and for the cause of Negro emancipation
and education. One of his best-known pro-Negro writings was ' The
Wonderful Crow', a poem included in his book, The Music Lesson
of Confucius. He was also a tireless student of Etruscan and Roman
antiquities, of the gipsies, of folklore, and magic—see his book,
Aradia, or ' The Gospel of the Witches'. He served in the American
Civil War, and came to Europe in 1869 and lived for about ten years
in London. He died in Florence in 1903.*

*Most of his books are now out of print and practically unobtain-
able. The following verses are two of the best examples of the quaint-
ness and charm of his poetry.*

## PING-WING

Ping-Wing he pie-man son,
He velly worst chilo allo Can-tón,
He steal he mother picklum mice,
An thlowee cat in bilin' rice.
Hab chow-chow up, an' 'Now,' talk he
'My wonda' where he meeow cat be?'

Ping-Wing he look-see, tinkey fun
Two piecee man who shleep in sun,
Shleepee sound he yeung-ki, fátha,
Ping tie 'um pigtail allo togata,
T'hen filee clacker an' offy lun,
T'hat piecee velly bad pie-man son.

Ping-Wing see gentleum wailo-go
He scleamee, '*Hai yah—fan-kwei lo!*'
All-same you savvy in Chinee,
'One foleign devil lookee see!'
But gentleum t'hat pidgin know,

He catchee Ping and floggum so,
T'hat állo-way flom t'hat day, maskee
He velly good littee Chinee.

*Note. Dis no pukka stoly. No hab got one so-bad piecee boy allo*
*China-side wat makee so he fátha. (Ah Chung)*

CHARLES G. LELAND: 1824–1903

Chow-chow: ate.      Yeung-ki: uncle.      Fátha: father.


## AHONG AND THE MUSQUITO

Supposey you make listen, my sing one piecee song,
My make he first-chop fashion about the glate Ahong;
He blavest man in China-side, or any side about;
My bettee you five dolla! *hai!* he blavest party out.

He only fightee 'skeeta, you tinkee t'hat not much.
No hab one Manchu Tartar t'hat kali fightee such.
My lather fightee dlagon that killee allo dead——
T'hat 'skeeta Ahong killee top-side he Empelor's head! . . .

CHARLES G. LELAND

Glate: great.      Kali: care to.      Allo: all.


## NEXT TO OF COURSE GOD

'Next to of course god america i
love you land of the pilgrims and so forth oh
say can you see by the dawn's early my
country 'tis of centuries come and go
and are no more what of it we should worry
in every language even deafanddumb
thy sons acclaim your glorious name by gorry
by jingo by gee by gosh by gum

why talk of beauty what could be more beautiful than these heroic happy dead
who rushed like lions to the roaring slaughter
they did not stop to think they died instead
then shall the voice of liberty be mute?'

He spoke. And drank rapidly a glass of water.

E. E. CUMMINGS

From

## THE BOOK OF THE LAMENTATIONS OF THE POET MACGONAGALL

On yonder hill there stands a coo,
If it's no there, it's awa noo.

WILLIAM MACGONAGALL

## THE PARSONS

What's the gud of these Pazons? They're the most despard
  rubbage go'n',
Reg'lar humbugs they are. Show me a Pazon, show me a
  drone!
Livin' on the fat of the land, livin' on the people's money
The same's the drones is livin' on the beeses honey.

T. E. BROWN

## UNCULTIVATED ACCENT

The Dago, the Injun, the Chink, the Jew,
The Darkie, the Parsee pale,
They *spik-a de Eengleesh* unlike you——
O Pedigree-parasite, Thoroughbred's-tail,

[33]

With accent pickled in Oxford ale——
But the faces and races 'beyond the pale',
Are *they* so funny—or *you*?

INCOGNITO

## Cockney Rhymes

### EPITAPH ON A 'MARF'

Wot a marf 'e'd got,
Wot a marf.
When 'e wos a kid,
Goo' Lor' luv'll
'Is pore old muvver
Must 'a' fed 'im wiv a shuvvle.

Wot a gap 'e'd got,
Pore chap,
'E'd never been known to larf,
'Cos if 'e did
It's a penny to a quid
'E'd 'a' split 'is fice in 'arf.

TRADITIONAL

### 'BIBY'S' EPITAPH

A muvver was barfin' 'er biby one night,
The youngest of ten and a tiny young mite,
The muvver was poor and the biby was thin,
Only a skelington covered in skin;

[34]

The muvver turned rahnd for the soap off the rack,
She was but a moment, but when she turned back,
The biby was gorn; and in anguish she cried,
'Oh, where is my biby?'—The angels replied:

'Your biby 'as fell dahn the plug-'ole,
Your biby 'as gorn dahn the plug;
The poor little thing was so skinny and thin
'E oughter been barfed in a jug;
Your biby is perfeckly 'appy,
'E won't need a barf any more,
Your biby 'as fell dahn the plug-'ole,
Not lorst, but gorn before.'

ANON

## HIGHER EDUCATION

As I was laying on the green
A little book it chanced I seen.
Carlyle's *Essay on Burns* was the edition——
I left it laying in the same position.

ANON

## THE BLEED'N' SPARRER

We 'ad a bleed'n' sparrer wot
Lived up a bleed'n' spaht,
One day the bleed'n' rain came dahn
An' washed the bleeder aht.

An' as 'e layed 'arf drahnded
Dahn in the bleed'n' street

[35]

'E begged that bleed'n' rainstorm
To bave 'is bleed'n' feet.

But then the bleed'n' sun came aht——
Dried up the bleed'n' rain——
So that bleed'n' little sparrer
'E climbed up 'is spaht again.

But, Oh!—the crewel sparrer'awk,
'E spies 'im in 'is snuggery,
'E sharpens up 'is bleed'n' claws
An' rips 'im aht by thuggery!

Jist then a bleed'n' sportin' type
Wot 'ad a bleed'n' gun
'E spots that bleed'n' sparrer'awk
An' blasts 'is bleed'n' fun.

.    .    .    .    .

The moral of this story
Is plain to everyone——
That them wot's up the bleed'n' spaht
Don't get no bleed'n' fun.

ANON

*All this reminds one that the Great Exhibition of 1851 was housed
in the Crystal Palace, which also housed the great tree, the Sibthorp
Elm. When Queen Victoria asked the Duke of Wellington what
could be done about the rude behaviour of the sparrows in the elm,
he replied: 'Try sparrow-hawks, ma'am.'*

# The Voice of America

## THIRTY PURPLE BIRDS

Toity poiple boids
Sitt'n on der coib
A' choipin' and a' boipin
An' eat'n doity woims.

ANON (NEW YORK)

## THE BUDDING BRONX

Der spring is sprung
Der grass is riz
I wonder where dem boidies is?

Der little boids is on der wing,
Ain't dat absoid?
Der little wings is on der boid!

ANON (NEW YORK)

## SONG OF THE SPANISH-AMERICAN WAR

Oh! dewy was the morning upon the first of May,
And Dewey was the Admiral down in Manila Bay,
And dewy were the Spaniards' eyes—those orbs of
black and blue,
And dew we feel discouraged? I dew not think we
dew!

TRADITIONAL: U.S.A.

## THE FIRST BANJO

Go'way, fiddle! folks is tired o' hearin' you a-squawkin'——
Keep silence fur yo' betters!—don't you heah de banjo talkin'?
About de 'possum's tail she's gwine to lecter—ladies, listen!
About de ha'r whut isn't dar, an' why de ha'r is missin':

'Dar's gwine to be a' oberflow,' said Noah, lookin' solemn——
Fur Noah tuk the *Herald*, an' he read de ribber column——
An' so he sot his hands to wuk a-cl'arin' timber-patches,
An' 'lowed he's gwine to build a boat to beat de steamah
  *Natchez*.

Ol' Noah kep' a-nailin' an' a-chippin' an' a-sawin';
An' all de wicked neighbours kep' a-laughin' an' a-pshawin';
But Noah didn't min' 'em, knowin' whut wuz gwine to
  happen:
An' forty days an' forty nights de rain it kep' a-drappin',

Now, Noah had done cotched a lot ob ebry sort o' beas'es——
Ob all de shows a-trabbelin', it beat 'em all to pieces!
He had a Morgan colt an' sebral head o' Jarsey cattle——
An' druv 'em 'board de Ark as soon 's he heered de thunder
  rattle.

Den sech anoder fall ob rain!—it come so awful hebby,
De ribber riz immejitly, an' busted troo de lebbee;
De people all wuz drownded out—'cep' Noah an' de critters,
An' men he'd hired to work de boat—an' one to mix de
  bitters.

De Ark she kep' a-sailin' an' a-sailin', *an'* a-sailin';
De lion got his dander up, an' like to brik de palin';
De sarpints hissed; de painters yelled; tell, whut wid all de
    fussin',
You c'u'dn't hardly heah de mate a-bossin' roun' an' cussin'.

Now, Ham, he only nigger whut wuz runnin' on de packet,
Got lonesome in de barber-shop, and c'u'dn't stan' de racket;
An' so, fur to amuse he-se'f, he steamed some wood an' bent
    it,
An' soon he had a banjo made—de fust dat wuz invented.

He wet de ledder, stretched it on; made bridge an' screws an'
    aprin';
An' fitted in a proper neck—'twas berry long and tap'rin';
He tuk some tin, an' twisted him a thinble fur to ring it;
An' den de mighty question riz: how wuz he gwine to string
    it?

De 'possum had as fine a tail as dis dat I's a-singin';
De ha'r's so long an' thick an' strong—des fit fur banjo-
    stringin';
Dat nigger shaved 'em off as short as wash-day-dinner graces;
An' sorted ob 'em by de size, f'om little E's to basses.

He strung her, tuned her, struck a jig—'twus 'Nebber min' de
    wedder'——
She soun' like forty-lebben bands a-playin' all togedder;
Some went to pattin'; some to dancin': Noah called de figgers;
An' Ham he sot an' knocked de tune, de happiest ob niggers!

Now, sence dat time—it's mighty strange—dere's not de
slightes' showin'

Ob any ha'r at all upon de 'possum's tail a-growin';
An' curi's, too, dat nigger's ways: his people nebber los'
 'em——
Fur whar you finds de nigger—dar's de banjo an' de 'possum!

IRWIN RUSSELL

## DIXIE

I wish I was in de land ob cotton,
Ole times dar am not forgotten;
In Dixie land whar' I was bawn in
'Arly on a frosty mawnin'.

Ole missus marry Will de Weaber;
Will he was a gay deceaber;
When he put his arms around her,
He looked as fierce as a forty-pounder.

His face was sharp as a butcher's cleaber,
But dat didn't seem a bit to greabe her.
Will run away, missus to a decline,
Her face was de colour ob de bacon rine.

When missus libbed, she libbed in clober,
When she died she died all ober;
How could she act de foolish part,
An' marry a man to break her heart?

Buckwheat cakes and cornmeal batter
Makes you fat, or little fatter;
Here's de health to de next ole missus,
An' all de gals as wants to kiss us.

[40]

Now if you want to drive away sorrow,
Come and hear dis song to-morrow;
Den hoe it down, and scratch de grabble,
To Dixie land I'm bound to trabble.

*Chorus*
I wish I was in Dixie land, hooray! hooray!
   In Dixie land
   We'll take our stand
To live and die in Dixie.
Away, away, away down Souf in Dixie.
Away, away, away down Souf in Dixie.

**ANON**

*This, in the original wording of the famous song, 'Dixie', first appeared in* The New Orleans Times-Democrat *some years before the American Civil War. The song, as sung during the war, was a slight variation of the above.*

# Potted Biography

\* \* \* \* \* \* \* \* \* \* \* \* \* \* \* \* \* \* \* \* \* \* \* \* \*

*In days of old when knights were bold, and folks had time to read and rhyme—there was popular demand for the long poem weaving the chequered career of certain nitwits or misfits who lived by their wits. Typically, topically gay was the turncoat Vicar of Bray, incumbent of a Berkshire parsonage who was, in fact, a real personage. This song was written (so they say) in George I's plum-pudding day, by an unknown Ensign who sang his tunes in Colonel Fuller's troop of dragoons.*

*A few such rhyming histories follow—heartlessly lopped from a hundred and thirty verses to a modest thirteen, or thereabouts, to suit the modern taste for briefs, shorts and snacks.*

*The briefest of all potted biographies turned out to-day are the Clerihews—so named after their original creator, E. C. (for Clerihew) Bentley. Max Beerbohm's earlier efforts were amusing, too, but the great charm of the Clerihew is in its succinct accuracy as biography. Almost the best known was 'Sir Christopher Wren'. This, and his others, have appeared in print so often that they are not included here; instead, I am quoting a few new ones (not by Bentley) which I am calling, Mock-Clerihews, Near-Clerihews and Non-Clerihews.*

### NELL GWYNNE

When Charles II
Beckon'd
Nell

Fell!          RUTH SILCOCK

## CALIGULA

The Emperor Caligula
's Habits were somewhat irrigula.
When he sat down to lunch
He got drunk at onch.

ROBERT LONGDEN

## CLAUDIUS

The Emperor Claudius
Used to keep a baudius.
When he got more criminal
He ran a den on the Viminal.

ROBERT LONGDEN

## THE HOLY ROMAN EMPIRE
### THE LIVES OF THE POPES

Dr. Marie Stopes,
After reading the Lives of the Popes,
Remarked: 'What a difference it would have made
    to these Pages
If I had been born in the Middle Ages.'

THE HON. MRS. GEOFFREY EDWARDS

## QUEEN ELIZABETH

Oh dearest Bess
I like your dress;
Oh sweetest Liz
I like your phiz;

[43]

Oh dearest Queen
I've never seen
A face more like
A soup-tureen.

ANON

## KING CHARLES II

Here lies our mutton-eating King
    Whose word no man relies on,
Who never said a foolish thing,
    Nor ever did a wise one.

JOHN WILMOT, EARL OF ROCHESTER

*The above is the original, and more insulting version. But Charles, of course, had his usual last word when he said: 'My sayings are my own, my actions are my ministers'!'*

## HELEN

Helen of Troy,
See the Heroes deploy!
'Ship Ahoy! Attaboy!'
Shout the low οἱ πολλοί.

ARD SLOK

## HO-HO OF THE GOLDEN BELT
### LINES FROM ONE OF THE 'NINE STORIES OF CHINA'

A beautiful maiden was little Min-Ne,
Eldest daughter of wise Wang-ke;
Her skin had the colour of saffron-tea,
And her nose was flat as flat could be;

And never was seen such beautiful eyes,
Two almond-kernels in shape and size,
Set in a couple of slanting gashes,
And not in the least disfigured by lashes;
  And then such feet!
  You'd scarcely meet
In the longest walk through the grandest street
  (And you might go seeking
  From Nanking to Peking)
A pair so remarkably small and neat.

  Two little stumps,
  Mere pedal lumps,
That toddle along with the funniest thumps,
In China, you know, are reckon'd trumps.
It seems a trifle, to make such a boast of it;
  But how they *will* dress it:
  And bandage and press it,
By making the least, to make the most of it!

  As you may suppose,
  She had plenty of beaux
Bowing around her beautiful toes,
Praising her feet, and eyes, and nose
In rapturous verse and elegant prose!
She had lots of lovers, old and young;
There was lofty Long, and babbling Lung,
Opulent Tin, and eloquent Tung,
Musical Sing, and, the rest among,
Great Hang-Yu and Yu-be-Hung.

But though they smiled, and smirk'd and bow'd,
None could please her of all the crowd;

Lung and Tung she thought too loud;
Opulent Tin was much too proud;
Lofty Long was quite too tall;
Musical Sing sung very small;
And, most remarkable freak of all,
Of great Hang-Yu the lady made game,
And Yu-be-Hung she mock'd the same,
By echoing back his ugly name!

But the hardest heart is doom'd to melt;
Love is a passion that *will* be felt;
And just when scandal was making free
To hint 'What a pretty old maid she'd **be**',—
    Little Min-Ne,
    Who but she?
Married Ho-Ho of the Golden Belt!
A man, I must own, of bad reputation,
And low in purse, though high in station——
A sort of Imperial poor relation,
Who rank'd as the Emperor's second cousin
Multiplied by a hundred dozen;
And, to mark the love the Emperor felt,
    Had a pension clear
    Of three pounds a year,
And the honour of wearing a Golden Belt! . . .

Yet how he managed to win Min-Ne
The men declared they couldn't see;
But all the ladies, over their tea,
In this one point were known to agree:
*Four gifts* were sent to aid his plea:
A smoking-pipe with a golden clog,
A box of tea and a poodle dog,

And a painted heart that was all a-flame,
And bore, in blood, the lover's name.
Ah! how could presents pretty as these
A delicate lady fail to please?
She smoked the pipe with the golden clog
And drank the tea, and ate the dog,
And kept the heart,—and that's the way
The match was made, the gossips say.


I can't describe the wedding-day,
Which fell in the lovely month of May,
Nor stop to tell of the Honey-moon,
And how it vanish'd all too soon;
Alas! that I the truth must speak,
And say that in the fourteenth week,
Soon as the wedding guests were gone,
And their wedding suits began to doff,
Min-Ne was weeping and 'taking-on',
For *he* had been trying to 'take her off'.


Six wives before he had sent to heaven,
And being partial to number 'seven',
He wish'd to add his latest pet,
Just, perhaps, to make up the set!
Mayhap the rascal found a cause
Of discontent in a certain clause
In the Emperor's very liberal laws,
Which gives, when a Golden Belt is wed,
Six hundred pounds to furnish the bed;
And if in turn he marry a score,
With every wife six hundred more. . . .

At last Ho-Ho, the treacherous man,
Contrived the most infernal plan
Invented since the world began;
He went and got him a savage dog,
Who'd eat a woman as soon as a frog;
Kept him a day without any prog,
Then shut him up in an iron bin,
Slipp'd the bolt and lock'd him in;
 Then giving the key
 To poor Min-Ne,
Said, 'Love there's something you *mustn't* see
In the chest beneath the orange tree'.

.   .   .   .   .   .

Poor mangled Min-Ne! with her latest breath
She told her father the cause of her death;
And so it reach'd the Emperor's ear,
And his highness said, 'It is very clear
Ho-Ho has committed a murder here!'
And he doom'd Ho-Ho to end his life
By the terrible dog that kill'd his wife;
But in mercy (let his praise be sung!)
His thirteen brothers were merely hung,
And his slaves bamboo'd in the mildest way,
For a calendar month, three times a day.
And that's the way that Justice dealt
With wicked Ho-Ho of the Golden Belt!
JOHN G. SAXE: 1816–87

## NONGTONGPAW

John Bull for pastime took a prance,
Some time ago, to peep at France;

To talk of sciences and arts,
And knowledge gain'd in foreign parts.
Monsieur, obsequious, heard him speak,
And answer'd John in heathen Greek:
To all he ask'd, 'bout all he saw,
'Twas, *Monsieur, je vous n'entends pas.*

John, to the Palace Royal come,
Its splendour almost struck him dumb.
'I say, whose house is that there here?'
'House! *Je vous n'entends pas, Monsieur.*
'What, Nongtongpaw again!' cries John;
'This fellow is some mighty Don:
No doubt he's plenty for the maw,
I'll breakfast with this Nongtongpaw.'

John saw Versailles from Marli's height,
And cried, astonish'd at the sight,
'Whose fine estate is that there here?'
'State! *Je vous n'entends pas, Monsieur.*'
His? What! the land and houses too?
The fellow's richer than a Jew:
On everything he lays his claw!
I should like to dine with Nongtongpaw.'

Next tripping came a courtly fair,
John cried, enchanted with her air,
'What lovely wench is that there here!'
'*Ventch! Je vous n'entends pas, Monsieur.*'
'What, he again? Upon my life!
A palace, lands, and then a wife
Sir Joshua might delight to draw:
I should like to sup with Nongtongpaw.

[49]

'But hold! whose funeral's that?' cries John.
*Je vous n'entends pas.*—'What, is he gone?
Wealth, fame, and beauty could not save
Poor Nongtongpaw then from the grave!
His race is run, his game is up—
I'd with him breakfast, dine and sup;
But since he chooses to withdraw,
Good night t'ye, Mounseer Nongtongpaw!'

CHARLES DIBDIN: 1745–1813

*Charles Dibdin, musician, actor, theatrical manager, and poet, was the great song-writer of the Navy. Among hundreds of compositions he wrote 'Heart of Oak' ('Come cheer up my lads 'tis to glory we steer'), 'Tom Bowling', and other still popular songs.*

## THE STORY OF SAMUEL JACKSON

I'll tell you of a sailor now, a tale that can't be beat,
His name was Samuel Jackson, and his height was seven feet;
And how this man was shipwrecked in the far Pacific Isles,
And of the heathen natives with their supposititious wiles.

Now when the others cut the ship, because she was a wreck,
They left this Samuel Jackson there, a-standin' on the deck—
That is, a standin' on the deck, while sittin' on the boom;
They wouldn't let him in the boat 'cos he took up too much room.

When up there came a tilted wave, and like a horse it romped,
It fell like mountains on the boat, and so the boat was swamped;
And of those selfish mariners full every one was drowned,
While Samuel, standing on the deck, beheld it safe and sound.

[50]

Now when the sea grew soft and still, and all the gale was o'er.
Sam Jackson made himself a raft, and paddled safe ashore.
For fear of fatal accidents—not knowin' what might come,
He took a gun and matches, with a prudent cask of rum.

Now this island where he landed proved as merry as a fife,
For its indigents had ne'er beheld a white man in their life;
Such incidents as rum and guns they never yet had seen,
And likewise, in religion, they were awful jolly green.

But they had a dim tradition, from their ancestors, in course,
Which they had somehow *de*rived from a very ancient source:
How that a god would come to them, and set the island right;
And how he should be orful tall, and likewise pearly white.

Now when they saw this Samuel approachin' on his raft,
The news through all the island shades was quickly telegraft,
How all their tribulat-i-ons would speedily be past,
'Cos the long-expected sucker was invadin' 'em at last.

Now when Sam Jackson stept ashore, as modest as you please,
Nine thousand bloomin' savages received him on their knees;
He looked around in wonderment, regardin' it as odd,
Not bein' much accustomed to be worshipped as a god.

But he twigged the situation, and with a pleasin' smile
Stretched out his hands, a-blessin' all the natives of the isle;
He did it well, although his paws were bigger than a pan,
Because he was habitual a most politeful man.

So to return their manners, and nary-wise for fun,
He raised himself with dignity, and then fired off his gun:

So all allowed that he must be one of the heavenly chaps,
Since he went about with lightning and dispensed with
    thunderclaps.

They took him on their shoulders, and he let it go for good,
And went into their city in the which a temple stood,
And sot him on the altar, and made him their salams,
And brought him pleasant coco-nuts, with chickens, po and
    yams.

And from that day henceforward, in a captivating style,
He relegated, as he pleased, the natives of that isle;
And when an unbeliever rose—as now and then were some,
He cured their irreligion with a little taste of rum.

He settled all their business, and he did it very well,
So everything went booming like a blessed wedding bell;
Eleven lovely feminines attended to his wants,
And a guard of honour followed him to all his usual haunts.

Now what mortal men are made of, that they can't put up
    with bliss,
I do not know, but this I know, that Sam got tired of this;
He wished that he was far away, again aboard a ship,
And all he thought of—night and day—was givin' 'em the
    slip.

And so one night when all was still and every soul asleep,
He got into a good canoe and paddled o'er the deep,
But oh the row the natives made, when early in the morn
They came to worship Samuel, and found their god was gone!

Then Samuel travelled many days, but had the luck at last
To meet a brig from Boston where he shipped before the
    mast;
And he gave it as his sentiments, and no one thought it odd,
He was better off as sailor than when sailing as a god.

Now many years had flown away when Samuel was forgot,
There came a ship for pearl shell unto that lonely spot;
They went into the temple, and what do you suppose
They found the natives worshipping—a suit of Samuel's
    clothes!

And this was the tradition of the people of the soil,
How once a great divinity had ruled upon their isle;
Four fathoms tall, with eyes like fire, and such was their
    believin',
One night he got upon the moon—and sailed away to Heaven!

CHARLES G. LELAND

## THE ANNUITY

    I gaed to spend a week in Fife—
        An unco week it proved to be—
    For there I met a waesome wife
        Lamentin' her viduity.
    Her grief brak out sae fierce and fell,
    I thought her heart wad burst the shell;
    And—I was sae left to mysel'—
        I sell't her an annuity.

    The bargain lookit fair enough—
        She just was turn'd o' saxty-three—

[53]

I couldna guess'd she'd prove sae teugh
   By human ingenuity.
But years have come, and years have gone,
And there she's yet as stieve's a stane—
The Limmer's growin' young again,
   Since she got her annuity.


She's crined awa' to bane an' skin.
   But that it seems is nought to me.
She's like to live—although she's in
   The last stage o' tenuity.
She munches wi' her wizen'd gums,
An' stumps about on legs o' Thrums,
But comes—as sure as Christmas comes—
   To ca' for her annuity.


I read the tables drawn wi' care
   For an Insurance Company;
Her chance o' life was stated there
   Wi' perfect perspicuity.
But tables here or tables there,
She's lived ten years beyond her share,
An's like to live a dozen mair,
   To ca' for her annuity.


Last Yule she had a fearfu' hoast—
   I thought a kink might set me free—
I led her out, 'mang snaw and frost,
   Wi' constant assiduity.
But Deil ma' care—the blast gaed by,
And miss'd the auld anatomy;
It just cost me a tooth, forbye
   Discharging her annuity.

If there's a sough o' cholera
Or typhus—wha sae gleg as she!
She buys up baths an' drugs, an' a',
    In siccan superfluity!
She doesna need—she's fever proof—
The pest walk'd o'er her very roof—
She tauld me sae—an' then her loof
    Held out for her annuity.


Ae day she fell—her arm she brak—
A compound fracture as could be—
Nae Leech the cure wad undertak,
Whate'er was the gratuity.
It's cured!—She handles't like a flail—
It does as weel in bits as hale—
But I'm a broken man mysel,
    Wi' her and her annuity.


Her broozled flesh and broken banes,
    Are weel as flesh an' banes can be.
She beats the taeds that live in stanes,
    An fatten in vacuity!
They die when they're exposed to air—
They canna thole the atmosphere—
But her!—expose her onywhere—
    She lives for her annuity.


If mortal means could nick her thread,
    Sma' crime it wad appear to me—
Ca't murder—or ca't homicide—
I'd justify't—an' do it tae.

But how to fell a wither'd wife
That's carved out o' the tree o' life—
The timmer limmer daurs the knife
   To settle her annuity.

I'd try a shot—But whar's the mark?—
   Her vital parts are hid frae me.
Her back-bane wanders through her sark
   In an unkenn'd corkscrewity.
She's palsified—an' shakes her head
Sae fast about, ye scarce can see't—
It's past the power o' steel or lead
   To settle her annuity.

She might be drown'd;—but go she'll not
   Within a mile o' loch or sea;—
Or hang'd if cord could grip a throat
   O' siccan exiguity.
It's fitter far to hang the rope—
It draws out like a telescope—
'Twad tak a dreadfu' length o' drop
   To settle her annuity.

Will puzion do't?—It has been tried.
   But, be't in hash or fricassee,
That's just the dish she can't abide,
   Whatever kind o' *goût* it hae.
It's needless to assail her doubts—
She gangs by instinct—like the brutes—
An' only eats an' drinks what suits
   Hersel' and her annuity.

The Bible says the age o' man
   Threescore and ten perchance may be.
She's ninety-four—Let them wha can
   Explain the incongruity.
She should hae lived afore the flood—
She's come o' Patriarchal blood—
She's some auld Pagan mummified
   Alive for her annuity.

She's been embalm'd inside and out—
   She's sautéd to the last degree—
There's pickle in her very snout
   Sae caper-like an' cruety,
Lot's wife was fresh compared to her—
They've Kyanized the useless knir—
She canna decompose—nae mair
   Than her accursed annuity.

The water-drap wears out the rock
As this eternal jaud wears me.
I could withstand the single shock,
   But not the continuity.
It's pay me here—an' pay me there—
An' pay me, pay me, evermair—
I'll gang demented wi' despair—
   I'm *charged* for her annuity.

GEORGE OUTRAM: ?  —1856

| | | |
|---|---|---|
| Teugh: tough. | Stieve: firm. | Crined: shrunk. |
| Thrums: threads | Hoast: cough. | Kink: paroxysm. |
| Forbye; besides. | Sough: whisper | Gleg: sharp. |
| Loof: hand. | Broozled: bruised. | Taeds: toads. |
| Thole: endure. | Puzion: poison. | Knir: witch |

The timmer limmer daurs: the wooden hussy dares.

# Philosophical and Metaphysical, Psychological and Sometimes Quizzical

★ ★ ★ ★ ★ ★ ★ ★ ★ ★ ★ ★ ★ ★ ★ ★ ★ ★ ★ ★ ★ ★

*Philosophy you must admit is rough on those who study it, so here's a Who's Who—not too long. Now you won't get the right names wrong.*

*Diogenes, so legends say, lived in his tub a life quite gay, till Alexander's shadow great o'ercast his will-to-meditate.*

*Socrates, Plato, Pythagoras, though wise, would talk too much, alas!*

*Great Aristotle had a lot o' little notions re emotions—These Bishop Berkeley thought unlarkly (B's views were nonsense, so Dr. Johnson swore in his rages. See Boswell's pages).*

*Now this effusion, you should find, gives Berkeley's views on form and mind:*

A philosopher—one, Bishop Berkeley—
Remarked, metaphysic'lly, darkly,
   'Quite half that we see
   Cannot possibly be
And the rest's altogether unlarkly.'

*Then, Kant loved Kant and loved not Man; but Coué said, 'I think I can' . . . so here are rhymes on thinking's terrors and some on wisdom's one-time errors; while others picture fading hope—as witness Alexander Pope:*

Some have for wits, and then for poets passed,
Turned critic next and proved plain-fool at last.

> But great ones grapple with affairs of state,
> So let's return to men and moments great.

*Mr. Winston Churchill has been quoted, mistakenly, as the author of a verse entitled 'Fame'. I wrote to him about this and in reply received a kind message, from which the following is a quotation:*

'Mr. Churchill wishes me to thank you for your letter of December 12 about the verse which has been wrongly attributed to him. He heard it quoted as follows many years ago:

> 'The gates of Fame are open wide
>  Its halls are always full,
>  And some go in by the door called "Push"
>  And some by the door called "Pull" . . .'

[59]

## Four More Brief Beliefs

The cheese-mites asked how the cheese got there,
    And warmly debated the matter;
The orthodox said it came from the air,
    And the heretics said from the platter.

ANON

Some of the hurts you have cured,
    And the sharpest you still have survived,
But what torments of grief you endured
From evils which never arrived!

RALPH WALDO EMERSON<br>(FROM THE FRENCH)

The Bells of Hell go *ting-a-ling-a-ling*
    For you but not for me;
For me the angels *sing-a-ling-a-ling*—
'Oh Death! Where is thy *sting-a-ling-a-ling*—
    Oh Grave! Thy victory?'

ANON

Thrice armed is he who has his quarrel just,
But nine times he who gets his blow in fust!

ANON

Lines from

WANG-TI

Last year my look-see plum-t*l*ee
all-flower all-same he snow,·

[60]

This spling much plenty snowflake
    all-same he plum-tlee blow
He snowflake fallee, meltee, he led leaf
    turnee blown,
My makee first-chop sing-song how luck go
    uppy-down.

                 CHARLES G. LELAND

## THE 'SELY' FLY

Once musing as I sat,
And candle burning by,
When all were hushed, I might discern
A simple, sely fly;
That flew before mine eyes,
With free rejoicing heart,
And here and there with wings did play,
As void of pain and smart.
Sometime by me she sat
When she had played her fill;
And ever when she rested had
About she fluttered still.
When I perceived her well
Rejoicing in her place,
'O happy fly!' (quoth I), and eke
O worm in happy case!
Which of us two is best?
I that have reason? No:
But thou that reason art without,
And therefore void of woe' . . .

## ON A GARDENER

Could he forget his death? that every hour
Was emblemed to it by the fading flower:
Should he not mind his end? Yes, needs he must,
That still was conversant 'mongst beds of dust.
Then let no onyon in an handkercher
Tempt your sad eyes into a needless tear;
If he that thinks on death well lives and dies,
The gardener sure is gone to Paradise.

FROM 'WIT RESTORED': 1658

## CARELESS CONTENT

*John Byrom, who lived from 1691 to 1763, wrote felicitous verse
as full of good sense as of humour. Here are a few lines from a poem
of his, which also parodies the Elizabethans.*

I am content, I do not care,
   Wag as it will the world for me;
When fuss and fret was all my fare,
   I got no ground as I could see:
So when away my caring went,
I counted cost, and was content.

With more of thanks and less of thought,
   I strive to make my matters meet;
To seek what ancient sages sought,
   Physic and food in sour and sweet:
To take what passes in good part,
And keep the hiccups from the heart.

[62]

With good and gentle humour'd hearts,
   I choose to chat where'er I come,
Whate'er the subject be that starts:
   But if I get among the glum,
I hold my tongue to tell the truth,
And keep my breath to cool my broth. . . .


With whom I feast I do not fawn,
   Nor if the folks should flout me, faint:
If wonted welcome be withdrawn,
   I cook no kind of a complaint:
With none disposed to disagree,
But like them best who best like me.


Not that I rate myself the rule
   How all my betters should behave:
But fame shall find me no man's fool,
   Nor to a set of men a slave.
I love a friendship free and frank,
And hate to hang upon a hank.


Now taste and try this temper, sirs,
   Mood it and brood it in your breast—
Or if ye ween, for worldly stirs,
   That man does right to mar his rest,
Let *me* be deft and debonair.
I am content, I do not care.

             JOHN BYROM: 1691–1763

# On Greatness

## GREAT ACTIONS

Great actions are not always true sons
Of great and mighty resolutions.

SAMUEL BUTLER

## GREAT THINGS

Great things are done when men and mountains meet
This is not done by jostling in the street.

WILLIAM BLAKE

## GREAT VIRTUE

If Moral Virtue was Christianity
Christ's pretensions were all Vanity . . .
The Moral Christian is the Cause
Of the Unbeliever and his Laws.

WILLIAM BLAKE

Lines from

## THE BALLAD OF THE GREEN OLD MAN

Green were the emerald grasses which grew upon the plain,
And green too were the verdant boughs which rippled in the rain,
Far green likewise the apple hue which clad the distant hill,
But at the station sat a man who looked far greener still.

An ancient man, a boy-like man, a person mild and meek,
A being who had little tongue, and nary bit of cheek.
And while upon him pleasant-like I saw the ladies look,
He sat a-counting money in a brownsome pocket-book.


Then to him a policeman spoke: 'Unless you feel too proud,
You'd better stow away that cash while you're in this here
    crowd;
There's many a chap about this spot who'd clean you out like
    ten.'
'And can it be,' exclaimed the man, 'there are such wicked
    men?'


Then up and down the platform promiscuous he strayed,
Amid the waiting passengers he took his lemonade,
A-making little kind remarks unto them all at sight,
Until he met two travellers who looked cosmopolite.


Now even as the old was green, this pair were darkly-brown;
They seemed to be of that degree which sports about the
    town.
Amid terrestrial mice, I ween, their destiny was Cat;
If ever men were gonoffs, I should say these two were that.


And they had watched that old man well with interested look,
And gazed him counting greenbacks in that brownsome
    pocket-book;
And the elder softly warbled with benevolential phiz,
'Green peas has come to market, and the veg'tables is riz. . . .'

---

Gonoff: a scriptural term for a Member of the Legislature or suchlike. A thief.

And the old man to the strangers very affable let slip
How that zealousy policeman had given him the tip,
And how his cash was buttoned in his pocket dark and dim,
And how he guessed no man alive on earth could gammon
    him.

In ardent conversation ere long the three were steeped,
And in that good man's confidence the younger party deeped.
The p'liceman, as he shadowed them, exclaimed in blooming
    rage,
'They're stuffin' of that duck, I guess, and leavin' out the sage.'

He saw the game distinctly, and inspected how it took,
And watched the reappearance of that brownsome pocket-
    book,
And how that futile ancient, ere he buttoned up his coat,
Had interchanged, obliging-like, a greensome coloured note.

And how they parted tenderly, and how the happy twain
Went out into the Infinite by taking of the train;
Then up the blue policeman came, and said: 'My ancient son,
Now you have gone and did it; say what you have been and
    done?'

And unto him the good old man replied with childish glee,
'They were as nice a two young men as I did ever see;
But they were in such misery their story made me cry;
So I lent 'em twenty dollars—which they'll pay me by-and-
    by.

'But as I had no twenty, we also did arrange,
They got from me a fifty bill, and gimme thirty change;

But they will send that fifty back, and by to-morrow's
    train——'
'That note,' out cried the constable, 'you'll never see again.'

'And that,' exclaimed the sweet old man, 'I hope I never may,
Because I do not care a cuss how far it keeps away;
For if I'm a judge of money, and I *reether* think I am,
The one I shoved was never worth a continental dam.

'They hev wandered with their sorrers into the sunny South.
They hev got uncommon swallows and an extry lot of mouth.
In the next train to the North'ard I expect to widely roam,
And if any come inquirin', jist say I ain't at home.'

The p'liceman lifted up his glance unto the sunny skies,
I s'pose the light was fervent, for a tear were in his eyes,
And said, 'If in your travels a hat store you should see,
Just buy yourself a beaver tile and charge that tile to me.' . . .

CHARLES G. LELAND

## THE SABBATH

Better a man ne'er be born
Than he trims his nails on a Sunday morn.

WARWICKSHIRE: TRADITIONAL

## RESPONSIBILITY

'Tis easy enough to be twenty-one:
'Tis easy enough to marry;
But when you try both games at once
'Tis a bloody big load to carry.

THE MIDLANDS: TRADITIONAL

## THE FORTUNES OF WAR

The fortunes of war I tell you plain
Are a wooden leg, or a golden chain.

TIME OF THE CRIMEAN WAR: TRADITIONAL

## THE BALANCE OF POWER

Now Europe balanced, neither side prevails;
For nothing's left in either of the scales.

ALEXANDER POPE: 1688–1744

## THE IRON CURTAIN

On Nevski Bridge a Russian stood
Chewing his beard for lack of food.
Said he, 'It's tough this stuff to eat
But a darn sight better than shredded wheat!'

ANON

## FIGHT FOR THE RIGHT

When a man hath no freedom to fight for at home,
Let him combat for that of his neighbours;
Let him think of the glories of Greece and of Rome,
And get knocked on the head for his labours.

To do good to mankind is the chivalrous plan,
And is always as nobly requited;
Then battle for freedom wherever you can,
And, if not shot or hang'd, you'll get Knighted.

BYRON

[68]

## NAPOLEON

Napoleon hoped that all the world would fall beneath his
  sway;
He failed in his ambition; and where is he to-day?
Neither the nations of the East nor the nations of the West
Have thought the thing Napoleon thought was to their
  interest.

ANON

## SPRINGTIME

'Tis dog's delight to bark and bite
And little birds to sing,
And if you sit on a red-hot brick
It's a sign of an early spring.      ANON

## EPITAPH—EPIGRAM

'Er as was 'as gone from we.
Us as is 'll go ter she.
**BLACK COUNTRY: TRADITIONAL**

## R.I.P.

Have you ever thought when a hearse goes by
That one fine day you were doomed to die?
They wrap you up in a big white sheet
And drop you down about thirteen feet.
The worms crawl in, and the worms crawl out,
The bugs play pinochle on your snout.
Your coffin rots and you turn to dust,
And that's the end of your life of lust.
**ANON: FROM CANADA**

## ANOTHER VERSION OF THE HEARSE SONG

The old Grey Hearse goes rolling by,
You don't know whether to laugh or cry;
For you know some day it will get you too,
And the hearse's next load may consist of you.

They'll take you out and they'll lower you down,
While men with shovels will stand all aroun';
They'll throw in dirt and they'll throw in rocks,
And they won't give a damn if they break the box.

And your eyes drop out and your teeth fall in,
And the worms crawl over your mouth and chin;
They invite their friends and their friends' friends too,
And you look like Hell when they're through with you.

ANON

## THE OPTIMIST AND THE PESSIMIST

The optimist, who always was a fool,
Cries, 'Look! My mug of ale is still half full.'
His brother gives the facts their proper twist—
'My mug's half empty!' sighs the pessimist.

ARNOLD SILCOCK

## PHILOSOPHY

Two men look out through the same bars;
One sees mud—and one sees stars.

FREDERICK LANGBRIDGE

## LAY NOT UP

The bees
Sneeze and wheeze
    Scraping pollen and honey
From the lime trees:

The ants·
Hurries and pants
    Storing up everything
They wants:

But the flies
Is wise
    When the cold weather comes
They dies.

L.W.G.

# Playtime on Parnassus: The Great Ones Relax

★ ★ ★ ★ ★ ★ ★ ★ ★ ★ ★ ★ ★ ★ ★ ★ ★ ★ ★ ★ ★ ★

*Nearly always when a great writer relaxes he lets himself go over the peccadilloes or puerilities of a fellow-writer—or a woman! The great, great-hearted, and great-girthed Dr. Johnson did both. His* Hermit Hoar *and* If a Man who Turnips Cries *were both imitations of other styles; and Peter Pindar then came along with a tit for tat. Later on Wordsworth wrote remarks about Shelley— and right away Lord Byron (and others) were very rude to Words-worth—and so it went on. Some of these rhyming take-offs follow.*

*But first of all here is the heavy-footed Dr. Johnson in a rare light-hearted mood.*

### THIRTY-FIVE

*Dr. Samuel Johnson, having called upon his amiable 'agreeable rattle', Mrs. Thrale, on her thirty-fifth birthday, was met with the complaint that none of her friends would send verses to her now she was thirty-five. Dr. Johnson's reply was immediately to improvise and recite the following rhyme, and to cap it by saying, 'And now you may see what it is to come for poetry to a dictionary maker; you may observe that the rhymes run in alphabetical order!'*

> Oft in danger, yet alive,
> We are come to thirty-five;

Long may better years arrive.
Better years than thirty-five.
Could philosophers contrive
Life to stop at thirty-five,
Time his hours should never drive
O'er the bounds of thirty-five.
High to soar, and deep to dive,
Nature gives at thirty-five.
Ladies, stock and tend your hive,
Trifle not at thirty-five;
For, howe'er we boast and strive,
Life declines from thirty-five;
He that ever hopes to thrive,
Must begin by thirty-five;
And all who wisely wish to wive,
Must look on Thrale at thirty-five!

SAMUEL JOHNSON: 1709–84

## LINES ON DR. JOHNSON

*Peter Pindar was the pen-name of the celebrated writer of humorous verse John Wolcot (1738–1819), some of whose verses are quoted in other chapters. This fragment shows how he weighed up the weighty doctor, though it is only poetic justice to add that Peter Pindar himself poured out a 'turgid' flood, most of which appears to-day to be more ponderous than humorous.*

I own I like not Johnson's turgid style,
That gives an inch th'importance of a mile;
Casts of manure a waggon-load around
To raise a simple daisy from the ground;
Uplifts the club of Hercules—for what?—
To crush a butterfly or brain a gnat;

Creatures a whirlwind from the earth to draw
A goose's feather or exalt a straw;
Sets wheels on wheels in motion—such a clatter:
To force up one poor nipperkin of water;
Bids ocean labour with tremendous roar,
To heave a cockle-shell upon the shore.
Alike in every theme his pompous art,
Heaven's awful thunder, or a rumbling cart!

PETER PINDAR: 1738–1819

*Here is another delicious 'sippet' to show that Dr. Johnson's style could change from the turgid and become as clear and refreshing as cold, amber beer:*

Hermit hoar, in solemn cell
    Wearing out life's evening grey;
Strike thy bosom, Sage, and tell
    What is bliss, and which the way.

Thus I spoke, and speaking sigh'd,
    Scarce repress'd the starting tear,
When the hoary sage reply'd,
    Come, my lad, and drink some beer!

SAMUEL JOHNSON

## ON A PAINTED WOMAN

To youths, who hurry thus away,
    How silly your desire is—
At such an early hour to pay
    Your compliments to Iris.

Stop, prithee, stop, ye hasty beaux,
No longer urge this race on;
Though Iris has put on her clothes,
She has not put her face on.

PERCY BYSSHE SHELLEY

## ABOUT THE SHELLEYS

'Twas not my wish
To be Sir Bysshe,
But 'twas the whim
Of my son Tim.

LINES QUOTED BY WORDSWORTH 1770–1850

## HE LIVED AMIDST TH' UNTRODDEN WAYS

### IMITATION OF WORDSWORTH

He lived amidst th' untrodden ways
    To Rydal Lake that lead;
A bard whom there were none to praise,
    And very few to read.

Behind a cloud his mystic sense,
    Deep hidden, who can spy?
Bright as the night when not a star
    Is shining in the sky.

Unread his works—his 'Milk White Doe'
    With dust is dark and dim;
It's still in Longman's shop, and oh!
    The difference to him!

HARTLEY COLERIDGE: 1796–1849

[75]

## ABOUT WORDSWORTH AND THE LAKE POETS

### INCLUDING LAMBE AND LLOYD

Yet let them not to vulgar Wordsworth stoop,
The meanest object of that lowly group,
Whose verse, of all but childish prattle void,
Seems blessed harmony to Lambe and Lloyd. . . .

LORD BYRON

## LAMB ON LAMB

*Charles Lamb did not love music. He could not, for he was tone deaf. Among some verses of his which recently came on the market was found one gem of self-revelation, as follows:*

Some cry up Haydn, some Mozart,
Just as the whim bites. For my part,
I do not care a farthing candle
For either of them, nor for Handel.

CHARLES LAMB: 1775–1834

## DIRCE

Stand close around, ye Stygian set,
  With Dirce in one boat conveyed!
Or Charon, seeing, may forget
  That he is old and she a shade.

WALTER SAVAGE LANDOR: 1775–1864

## ROBIN GOODFELLOW

*This poem on Puck—only a few lines of which are quoted here—has been attributed to Ben Jonson ('O Rare Ben Jonson'), but its actual authorship is still in doubt.*

When lads and lasses merry be,
    With possets and with junkets fine:
Unseen of all the company,
    I eat their cakes and sip their wine!
        And, to make sport,
        I puff and snort:
And out the candles I do blow:
        The maids I kiss,
        They shriek—Who's this?
    I answer naught, but ho, ho, ho!

When house or hearth doth sluttish lie,
    I pinch the maidens black and blue;
The bed-clothes from the bed pull I,
    And lay them naked all to view.
        'Twixt sleep and wake,
        I do them take,
And on the key-cold floor them throw;
        If out they cry,
        Then forth I fly,
    And loudly laugh out ho, ho, ho!

By wells and rills and meadows green,
    We nightly dance our heyday guise;
And to our fairy king and queen,
    We chant our moonlight minstrelsies.

When larks 'gin sing,
   Away we fling;
And babes new-born steal as we go;
   And elf in bed
   We leave instead,
And wend us laughing, ho, ho, ho!

ATTRIBUTED TO BEN JONSON:
1573?–1637

## SONG FROM 'THE WINTER'S TALE'

When daffodils begin to peer—
   With heigh! the doxy over the dale—
Why, then comes in the sweet o' the year,
   For the red blood reigns in the winter's pale.

The white sheet bleaching on the hedge—
   With heigh! the sweet birds, O, how they sing!—
Doth set my pugging tooth on edge,
   For a quart of ale is a dish for a king.

The lark, that tirra-lyra chants—
   With heigh! with heigh! the thrush and the jay—
Are summer songs for me and my aunts,
   While we lie tumbling in the hay.

WILLIAM SHAKESPEARE

## SONG FROM 'THE TEMPEST'

The master, the swabber, the boatswain, and I,
   The gunner, and his mate,
Lov'd Mall, Meg, and Marian, and Margery,
   But none of us car'd for Kate.

[78]

For she had a tongue with a tang,
  Would cry to a sailor, 'Go hang!'
She lov'd not the savour of tar nor of pitch;
Yet a tailor might scratch her where'er she did itch.
  Then to sea, boys, and let her go hang!

WILLIAM SHAKESPEARE

## THE BAIT

Come live with me, and be my love,
And we will some new pleasures prove
Of golden sands, and crystal brooks,
With silken lines and silver hooks.

There will the river whispering run
Warmed by thy eyes, more than the sun;
And there the enamoured fish will stay,
Begging themselves they may betray.

When thou wilt swim in that live bath,
Each fish, which every channel hath,
Will amorously to thee swim,
Gladder to catch thee, than thou him.

If thou, to be so seen, beest loath,
By sun or moon, thou darkenest both,
And if myself have leave to see,
I need not their light, having thee.

Let others freeze with angling reeds,
And cut their legs with shells and weeds,
Or treacherously poor fish beset,
With strangling snare, or windowy net.

[79]

Let coarse bold hands from slimy nest
The bedded fish in banks out-wrest;
Or curious traitors, sleeve-silk flies,
Bewitch poor fishes' wandering eyes.

For thee, thou need'st no such deceit,
For thou thyself art thine own bait:
That fish, that is not catched thereby,
Alas! is wiser far than I.

JOHN DONNE: 1573–1631

## CAUSE AND EFFECT

On his death-bed poor Lubin lies;
    His spouse is in despair;
With frequent sobs and mutual cries,
    They both express their care.

'A different cause,' says Parson Sly,
    'The same effect may give:
Poor Lubin fears that he may die;
    His wife, that he may live.'

MATTHEW PRIOR: 1664–1721

## EPIGRAM ON WIT

You beat your pate, and fancy wit will come;
Knock as you please, there's nobody at home!

ALEXANDER POPE: 1688–1744

### FISHERMEN AT DUSK

And now the salmon-fishers moist,
Their leathern boats begin to hoist;
And, like Antipodes in shoes,
Have shod their heads with their canoes.
How tortoise-like, but not so slow,
These rational amphibii go!
Let's in; for the dark hemisphere
Does now like one of them appear.

ANDREW MARVELL: 1621–78

### OH! ENGLAND!

Oh England full of sin but most of sloath
Spit out thy phlegm and fill thy breast with glory,
Thy gentry bleats, as if thy native cloth
Infused a sheepishness into their story,
Not that they all are so, but that the most
Are gone to grass and in the pasture lost.

GEORGE HERBERT: 1593–1633

### THE DRUNKEN SWINE

The drunkard now supinely snores,
His load of ale sweats through his pores,
Yet when he wakes the swine shall find,
A crapula remains behind.

CHARLES COTTON: SEVENTEENTH CENTURY

Verses from

## A NEW SONG OF NEW SIMILIES

Pert as a pear-monger I'd be
If Molly were but kind;
Cool as a cucumber could see
The rest of womankind.

Like a stuck pig I gaping stare,
And eye her o'er and o'er;
Lean as a rake with sighs and care,
Sleek as a mouse before.

Hard is her heart as flint or stone,
She laughs to see me pale;
And merry as a grig is grown,
And brisk as bottled ale.

Straight as my leg her shape appears;
O were we join'd together!
My heart would be scot-free from cares,
And lighter than a feather.

As soft as pap her kisses are,
Methinks I taste them yet;
Brown as a berry is her hair,
Her eyes as black as jet.

Brisk as a body-louse she trips,
Clean as a penny drest;
Sweet as a rose her breath and lips,
Round as the globe her breast.

Full as an egg was I with glee;
    And happy as a King.
Good Lord! how all men envy'd me!
    She lov'd like anything!

                    JOHN GAY: 1685–1732


# A FAREWELL TO LONDON, IN THE YEAR 1715

Dear, damn'd distracting town, farewell!
    Thy fools no more I'll tease:
This year in peace, ye critics, dwell,
    Ye harlots, sleep at ease!

Why should I stay? Both parties rage;
    My vixen mistress squalls;
The wits in envious feuds engage;
    And Homer (damn him!) calls.

Why make I friendships with the great,
    When I no favour seek?
Or follow girls seven hours in eight?
    I need but once a week.

Luxurious lobster-nights, farewell,
    For sober studious days!
And Burlington's delicious meal,
    For salads, tarts, and pease!

Adieu to all but Gay alone,
    Whose soul, sincere and free,
Loves all mankind, but flatters none,
    And so may starve with me.

                    ALEXANDER **POPE**

[83]

## TOBACCO

The pipe, with solemn interposing puff,
Makes half a sentence at a time enough;
The dozing sages drop the drowsy strain,
Then pause and puff, and speak, and pause again.
Such often, like the tube they so admire,
Important triflers! have more smoke than fire.
Pernicious weed! whose scent the fair annoys,
Unfriendly to society's chief joys,
The worst effect is banishing for hours
The sex whose presence civilizes ours.

WILLIAM COWPER: 1731–1800

## MARRIAGE

When a man has married a wife he finds out whether
Her knees and elbows are only glued together.

WILLIAM BLAKE: 1757–1827

## COLOGNE

In Köln, a town of monks and bones,
And pavements fang'd with murderous stones,
And rags, and hags, and hideous wenches;
I counted two and seventy stenches,
All well defined, and several stinks!
Ye Nymphs that reign o'er sewers and sinks,
The river Rhine, it is well known,
Doth wash your city of Cologne;
But tell me, Nymphs! What power divine
Shall henceforth wash the river Rhine?

## ON MY JOYFUL DEPARTURE FROM THE SAME CITY

As I am a rhymer,
And now at least a merry one,
Mr. Mum's Rudesheimer
And the church of St. Geryon
Are the two things alone
That deserve to be known
In the body and soul-stinking town
of Cologne.

SAMUEL TAYLOR COLERIDGE: 1772–1834

## EPIGRAM ON SINGERS

Swans sing before they die—'twere no bad thing
Should certain persons die before they sing.

SAMUEL TAYLOR COLERIDGE

# WHEN MOONLIKE ORE THE HAZURE
## SEAS

When moonlike ore the hazure seas
　　In soft effulgence swells,
When silver jews and balmy breaze
　　Bend down the Lily's bells;
When calm and deap, the rosy sleap
　　Has lapt your soal in dreams,
R Hangeline! R lady mine!
　　Dost thou remember Jeames?

I mark thee in the Marble All,
　　Where England's loveliest shine—
I say the fairest of them hall
　　Is Lady Hangeline.
My soul, in desolate eclipse,
　　With recollection teems—
And then I hask, with weeping lips,
　　Dost thou remember Jeames?

Away! I may not tell thee hall
　　This soughring heart endures—
There is a lonely sperrit-call
　　That Sorrow never cures;
There is a little, little Star,
　　That still above me beams;
It is the Star of Hope—but ar!
　　Dost thou remember Jeames?

WILLIAM MAKEPEACE THACKERAY:
1811–63

## WHEN A MAN'S BUSY

When a man's busy, why, leisure
Strikes him as wonderful pleasure:
Faith, and at leisure once is he?
Straightway he wants to be busy.

ROBERT BROWNING: 1812—89

## THE SHADES OF NIGHT

The shades of night were falling fast
And the rain was falling faster
When through an Alpine village passed
An Alpine village pastor.

A. E. HOUSMAN

# Parodies and Spites

\* \* \* \* \* \* \* \* \* \* \* \* \* \* \* \* \* \* \* \* \* \* \*

*The most horrid parodies are the most serious ones; serious, that is, in their playful treatment of a subject which should never be alluded to (especially in verse) except in deadly earnest.*

*The ghastliest parody I know is this:*

> Ring-a-ring-o'-geranium,
> A pocket full of uranium,
>     Hiro, shima,
> All fall down.

*That modern nursery-rhyme was the prize-winning entry by Robin A. Henderson, in an Observer newspaper competition held at Christmas, 1948.*

*And now.—So far as the rest of these parodies go, I have sometimes included a very old and well-known one, but always with a special purpose—generally because I have discovered new or little-known parodies of the same work, and need the odiferous comparison. ' I never nursed a dear gazelle', believe it or not, has six parodies!*

*Many parodies are purely spiteful in their damning, direct comment on the original. Others, at best, may be called caustic in their oblique allusion. Types of both bitter draughts are quoted.—Such are: ' An Unexpected Pleasure', lampooning Christina Rossetti, and ' Lovers and a Reflection', ridiculing the form (and the content) of Jean Ingelow's verse. Calverley, the culprit in the latter case, despite his ungallant action became on good terms with the Victorian poetess*

[88]

whose muse he had unmannerly manhandled. His biographer tells
us so. But it is very hard to believe.

Some parodies are what Sir John Squire calls 'Apes and Parrots':
others are more magnificent mummery, like his own parody of Gray's
'Elegy'. This, and 'How I Brought the Good News from Aix to
Ghent (or Vice Versa)' are, in their own right, versification of the
highest order, and memorable as two of the greatest classic laughter-
mixtures ever concocted. The latter is by the authors of '1066 and all
that'. And here it is:

## HOW I BROUGHT THE GOOD NEWS FROM AIX TO GHENT (OR VICE VERSA)

*It runs (or rather gallops) roughly as follows, we quote from
memory (having no boots of reference at hand),*

I sprang to the rollocks and Jorrocks and me,
And I galloped, you galloped, he galloped, we galloped
all three . . .
Not a word to each other; we kept changing place,
Neck to neck, back to front, ear to ear, face to face;
And we yelled once or twice, when we heard a clock
chime,
'Would you kindly oblige us, *Is that the right time?*'
As I galloped, you galloped, he galloped, we galloped, ye
galloped, they two shall have galloped; *let us trot.*

I unsaddled the saddle, unbuckled the bit,
Unshackled the bridle (the thing didn't fit)
And ungalloped, ungalloped, ungalloped, ungalloped a bit.
Then I cast off my bluff-coat, let my bowler hat fall,
Took off both my boots and my trousers and all—
Drank off my stirrup-cup, felt a bit tight,
And unbridled the saddle; it still wasn't right.

Then all I remember is, things reeling round
As I sat with my head 'twixt my ears on the ground—
For imagine my shame when they asked what I meant
And I had to confess that I'd been, gone and went
And *forgotten the news* I was bringing to Ghent,
Though I'd galloped and galloped and galloped and
    galloped and galloped
And galloped and galloped and galloped. (Had I not
    would have been galloped?)

ENVOI

So I sprang to a taxi and shouted 'To Aix!'
And he blew on his horn and he threw off his brakes,
And all the way back till my money was spent
We rattled and rattled and rattled and rattled and
    rattled
And rattled and rattled—
And eventually sent a telegram.

R. J. YEATMAN and W. C. SELLAR

# IF GRAY HAD HAD TO WRITE HIS ELEGY IN THE CEMETERY OF SPOON RIVER INSTEAD OF IN THAT OF STOKE POGES

The curfew tolls the knell of parting day,
  The whippoorwill salutes the rising moon,
And wanly glimmer in her gentle ray,
  The sinuous windings of the turbid Spoon.

Here where the flattering and mendacious swarm
  Of lying epitaphs their secrets keep,
At last incapable of further harm
  The lewd forefathers of the village sleep.

The earliest drug of half-awakened morn,
   Cocaine or hashish, strychnine; poppy-seeds
Or fiery produce of fermented corn
   No more shall start them on the day's misdeeds.

For them no more the whetstone's cheerful noise,
   No more the sun upon his daily course
Shall watch them savouring the genial joys,
   Of murder, bigamy, arson and divorce.

Here they all lie; and, as the hour is late,
   O stranger, o'er their tombstones cease to stoop,
But bow thine ear to me and contemplate
   The unexpurgated annals of the group.

There are two hundred only: yet of these
   Some thirty died of drowning in the river,
Sixteen went mad, ten others had D.T.s,
   And twenty-eight cirrhosis of the liver.

Several by absent-minded friends were shot,
   Still more blew out their own exhausted brains,
One died of a mysterious inward rot,
   Three fell off roofs, and five were hit by trains.

One was harpooned, one gored by a bull-moose,
   Four on the Fourth fell victims to lock-jaw,
Ten in electric chair or hempen noose
   Suffered the last exaction of the law.

Stranger, you quail, and seem inclined to run;
   But, timid stranger, do not be unnerved;

I can assure you that there was not one
   Who got a tithe of what he had deserved.

Full many a vice is born to thrive unseen,
   Full many a crime the world does not discuss,
Full many a pervert lives to reach a green
   Replete old age, and so it was with us.

Here lies a parson who would often make
   Clandestine rendezvous with Claflin's Moll,
And 'neath the druggist's counter creep to take
   A sip of surreptitious alcohol.

And here a doctor, who had seven wives,
   And, fearing this *ménage* might seem grotesque,
Persuaded six of them to spend their lives
   Locked in a drawer of his private desk.

And others here there sleep who, given scope,
   Had writ their names large on the Scrolls of
     Crime,
Men who, with half a chance, might haply cope,
   With the first miscreants of recorded time.

Doubtless in this neglected spot is laid
   Some village Nero who has missed his due,
Some Bluebeard who dissected many a maid,
   And all for naught, since no one ever knew.

Some poor bucolic Borgia here may rest
   Whose poisons sent whole families to their doom
Some hayseed Herod who, within his breast,
   Concealed the sites of many an infant's tomb.

Types that the Muse of Masefield might have
    stirred,
  Or waked to ecstasy Gaboriau,
Each in his narrow cell at last interred,
  All, all are sleeping peacefully below.

.     .     .     .     .     .

Enough, enough! But, stranger, ere we part,
  Glancing farewell to each nefarious bier,
This warning I would beg you to take to heart,
  'There is an end to even the worst career!'

                      SIR JOHN SQUIRE

## Lines from
# FOR A' THAT AND A' THAT
### IN IMITATION OF BURNS

A prince can make a belted knight
  A marquis, duke, and a' that,
And if the title's earned, all right,
  Old England's fond of a' that.
    For a' that, and a' that,
      Beales' balderdash, and a' that,
    A name that tells of service done
      Is worth the wear, for a' that.

Then let us pray that come it may
  And come it will for a' that,
That common sense may take the place
  Of common cant and a' that.

For a' that, and a' that,
  Who cackles trash and a' that,
Or be he lord, or be he low,
  The man's an ass for a' that.

SHIRLEY BROOKS: 1816—74

## THE HAPPY MAN

*A translation from the French of Gilles Ménage, who lived from
1613 to 1692. This poem probably inspired Oliver Goldsmith to
write the apparent parody, 'Madame Blaize', which is quoted on
the next page.*

La Pallisse was indeed, I grant,
  Not used to any dainty
When he was born—but could not want,
  As long as he had plenty.

His temper was exceeding good,
  Just of his father's fashion;
And never quarrels broil'd his blood,
  Except when in a passion.

O happy, happy is the swain
  The ladies so adore;
For many followed in his train,
  Whene'er he walk'd before.

Bright as the sun his flowing hair
  In golden ringlets shone;
And no one could with him compare,
  If he had been alone.

[94]

His talents I can not rehearse,
  But every one allows,
That whatsoe'er he wrote in verse,
  No one could call it prose.

His powerful logic would surprise,
  Amuse, and much delight:
He proved that dimness of the eyes
  Was hurtful to the sight.

He was not always right, 'tis true,
  And then he must be wrong;
But none had found it out, he knew,
  If he had held his tongue.

At last they smote him in the head—
  What hero ever fought all?
And when they saw that he was dead,
  They knew the wound was mortal.

And when at last he lost his breath,
  It closed his every strife;
For that sad day that seal'd his death,
  Deprived him of his life.


## AN ELEGY

### ON THE GLORY OF HER SEX, MRS. MARY BLAIZE

Good people all, with one accord,
  Lament for Madam Blaize,
Who never wanted a good word—
From those who spoke her praise.

The needy seldom pass'd her door,
    And always found her kind;
She freely lent to all the poor—
    Who left a pledge behind.

She strove the neighbourhood to please
With manners wondrous winning;
And never follow'd wicked ways—
    Unless when she was sinning.

At church, in silks and satins new,
    With hoop of monstrous size,
She never slumber'd in her pew—
    But when she shut her eyes.

Her love was sought, I do aver,
    By twenty beaux and more;
The King himself has follow'd her—
    When she has walk'd before.

But now, her wealth and finery fled,
    Her hangers-on cut short all;
The doctors found, when she was dead—
    Her last disorder mortal.

Let us lament, in sorrow sore,
    For Kent Street well may say,
That had she lived a twelvemonth more—
    She had not died to-day.

              **OLIVER GOLDSMITH: 1728–74**

## RIGID BODY SINGS

Gin a body meet a body
  Flyin' through the air,
Gin a body hit a body,
  Will it fly? and where?
Ilka impact has its measure,
  Ne'er a' ane hae I,
Yet a' the lads they measure me,
  Or, at least, they try.

Gin a body meet a body
  Altogether free,
How they travel afterwards
  We do not always see.
Ilka problem has its method
  By analytics high;
For me, I ken na ane o' them.
  But what the waur am I?

JAMES CLERK MAXWELL: 1831–79

## THE VILLAGE BLACKSMITH

Under a spreading gooseberry bush the village burglar lies,
The burglar is a hairy man with whiskers round his eyes
And the muscles of his brawny arms keep off the little flies.

He goes on Sunday to the church to hear the Parson shout.
He puts a penny in the plate and takes a pound note out
And drops a conscience-stricken tear in case he is found out.

ANON

[97]

## THE ARROW AND THE SONG
### A Shot at Random

I shot an arrow into the air:
I don't know how it fell or where;
But strangely enough, at my journey's end,
I found it again in the neck of a friend.

D. B. WYNDHAM LEWIS

## THE MODERN HIAWATHA
### From 'The Song of Milkanwatha'

When he killed the Mudjokivis,
Of the skin he made him mittens,
Made them with the fur side inside,
Made them with the skin side outside,
He, to get the warm side inside
Put the inside skin side outside;
He, to get the cold side outside,
Put the warm side fur side inside.
That's why he put fur side inside,
Why he put the skin side outside,
Why he turned them inside outside.

GEORGE A. STRONG

## AN UNEXPECTED PLEASURE

My heart is like one asked to dine
Whose evening dress is up the spout;
My heart is like a man would be
Whose raging tooth is half pulled out.
My heart is like a howling swell
Who boggles on his upper C;

My heart is madder than all these—
My wife's mamma has come to tea.

Raise me a bump upon my crown,
Bang it till green in purple dies;
Feed me on bombs and fulminates,
And turncocks of a medium size.
Work me a suit in crimson apes
And sky-blue beetles on the spree;
Because the mother of my wife
Has come—and means to stay with me.

ANON

## A BIRTHDAY

My heart is like a singing bird
    Whose nest is in a watered shoot:
My heart is like an apple-tree
    Whose boughs are bent with thickset fruit;
My heart is like a rainbow shell
    That paddles in a halcyon sea;
My heart is gladder than all these
    Because my love is come to me.

Raise me a dais of silk and down;
    Hang it with vair and purple dyes;
Carve it in doves and pomegranates,
    And peacocks with a hundred eyes;
Work it in gold and silver grapes,
    In leaves and silver fleurs-de-lys;
Because the birthday of my life
    Is come, my love is come to me.

CHRISTINA ROSSETTI: 18TH NOV. 1857

## A VALENTINE

The rose is red, the violet's blue
And pinks are sweet, and so are you.

*A traditional rhyme for St. Valentine's Day, from
Halliwell's 'Popular Rhymes'*

My nose is red, my lips are blue,
But gin is dearer far than you.

**ANON**

## LOVERS, AND A REFLECTION

IN MIMICRY OF THE VICTORIAN POETESS OF
THE JEAN INGELOW TYPE

In moss-prankt dells which the sunbeams flatter
  (And heaven it knoweth what that may mean;
Meaning, however, is no great matter)
  Where woods are a-tremble, with rifts atween;

Thro' God's own heather we wonn'd together,
  I and my Willie (O love my love);
I need hardly remark it was glorious weather,
  And flitterbats waver'd alow, above:

Boats were curtseying, rising, bowing,
  (Boats in that climate are so polite),
And sands were a ribbon of green endowing,
  And O the sundazzle on bark and bight!

Thro' the rare red heather we danced together,
  (O love my Willie!) and smelt for flowers
I must mention again it was gorgeous weather,
  Rhymes are so scarce in this world of ours:

[100]

By rises that flush'd with their purple favours,
   Thro' becks that brattled o'er grasses sheen,
We walked and waded, we two young shavers,
   Thanking our stars we were both so green.

We journeyed in parallels, I and Willie,
   In fortunate parallels! Butterflies,
Hid in weltering shadows of daffodilly
   Or marjoram, kept making peacock eyes:

Songbirds darted about, some inky
   As coal, some snowy (I ween) as curds;
Or rosy as pinks, or as roses pinky—
   They reck of no eerie To-come, those birds!

But they skim over bents which the millstream
    washes,
   Or hang in the lift 'neath a white cloud's hem;
They need no parasols, no goloshes;
   And good Mrs. Trimmer she feedeth them.

Then we thrid God's cowslips (as erst His heather)
   That endowed the wan grass with their golden
     blooms;
And snapt—(it was perfectly charming weather)—
   Our fingers at Fate and her goddess-glooms:

And Willie 'gan sing (O, his notes were fluty;
   Wafts fluttered them out to the white-wing'd
     sea)—
Something made up of rhymes that have done much
    duty,
   Rhymes (better to put it) of 'ancientry':

Bowers of flowers encounter'd showers
   In William's Carol—(O love my Willie!)
Then he bade sorrow borrow from blithe to-morrow
   I quite forget what—say a daffodilly:

A nest in a hollow, 'with buds to follow',
   I think occurred next in his nimble strain;
And clay that was 'kneaden' of course in Eden—
   A rhyme most novel, I do maintain:

Mists, bones, the singer himself, love-stories,
   And all least furlable things got 'furled';
Not with any design to conceal their 'glories',
   But simply and solely to rhyme with 'world'.

  .     .     .     .     .     .

O if billows and pillows and hours and flowers,
   And all the brave rhymes of an elder day,
Could be furled together, this genial weather,
   And carted, or carried on 'wafts' away,
Nor ever again trotted out—ah me!
   How much fewer volumes of verse there'd be!

C. S. CALVERLEY

*The original lines from 'The Fire Worshippers' by Thomas
Moore have inspired a large number of parodies, and a few of the
choicest follow:*

### DISASTER

'Twas ever thus from childhood's hour!
   My fondest hopes would not decay:
I never loved a tree or flower
   Which was the first to fade away!

The garden, where I used to delve
   Short-frock'd, still yields me pinks in
      plenty:
The pear tree that I climb'd at twelve
   I see still blossoming, at twenty.

I never nursed a dear gazelle;
   But I was given a perroquet—
(How I did nurse him if unwell!)
   He's imbecile, but lingers yet.
He's green, with an enchanting tuft;
   He melts me with his small black eye:
He'd look inimitable stuff'd,
   And knows it—but he will not die!

I had a kitten—I was rich
   In pets—but all too soon my kitten
Became a full-sized cat, by which
   I've more than once been scratch'd and bitten.
And when for sleep her limbs she curl'd
   One day beside her untouch'd plateful,
And glided calmly from the world,
   I freely own that I was grateful.

And then I bought a dog—a queen!
   Ah Tiny, dear departing pug!
She lives, but she is past sixteen
   And scarce can crawl across the rug.
I loved her, beautiful and kind;
   Delighted in her pert Bow-wow:
But now she snaps if you don't mind:
   'Twere lunacy to love her now.

[103]

I used to think, should e'er mishap
    Betide my crumple-visaged Ti,
In shape of prowling thief, or trap,
    Or coarse bull-terrier—I should die.
But ah! disasters have their use;
    And life might e'en be too sunshiny:
Nor would I make myself a goose,
    If some big dog should swallow Tiny.

C. S. CALVERLEY

## ANOTHER PARODY

I've never had a piece of toast
Particularly long and wide,
But fell upon the sanded floor,
And always on the buttered side.

JAMES PAYN

## THE ORIGINAL

### LINES FROM THE FIRE WORSHIPPERS

Oh! ever thus from childhood's hour,
I've seen my fondest hopes decay;
I never loved a tree or flower,
But 'twas the first to fade away.
I never nursed a dear gazelle,
To glad me with its soft black eye,
But when it came to know me well,
And love me, it was sure to die!

THOMAS MOORE: 1779–1852

## ANOTHER PARODY
### THEME WITH VARIATIONS

*I never loved a dear Gazelle—*
Nor anything that cost me much:
High prices profit those who sell,
But why should *I* be fond of such?

*To glad me with his soft black eye*
My son comes trotting home from school;
He's had a fight but can't tell why—
He always *was* a little fool!

*But, when he came to know me well,*
He kicked me out, her testy Sire:
And when I stained my hair, that Belle
Might note the change, and thus admire

*And love me, it was sure to dye*
A muddy green, or staring blue:
Whilst one might trace, with half an eye,
The still triumphant carrot through.

LEWIS CARROL

## ANOTHER PARODY
### 'TWAS EVER THUS

I never rear'd a young gazelle,
(Because, you see, I never tried);
But had it known and loved me well,
No doubt the creature would have died.

My rich and aged Uncle John
Has known me long and loves me well,
But still persists in living on—
I would he were a young gazelle.

H. S. LEIGH

## MEDITATION (IN AUTUMN)

The leaves are falling from the tree, which bodes the end of
you and me. Quite suddenly we'll fall off crash and lie uncon-
scious in the mash. This seems a little drear—but no, we need
not really make it so, and *Wilhelmina Stitch* can bring the
fragrance out of anything. For think how peaceful it will be
to lie insensate 'neath a tree; and how ennobling, ah, how big,
to be uprooted by a pig!

BRIDGET MULLER

## A FACT

I bought a chicken in the street and hung it up to serve as
meat; but when I came to view the bird, 'twas black and green
and looked absurd. Was I despondent? Never—no—your
*Wilhelmina's* never so, though I had lost my lunch, 'twas true,
and wasted five and sixpence too. I sat me down and took a
breath, thought fragrantly of Life and Death, of Strength and
Grace and Love and Power, and so I mused for half an hour.
Then up I rose, replete with calm, and softly sang the Hun-
dredth Psalm; I gave the chicken to my mother and sallied
forth to buy another.

BRIDGET MULLER

## SOFT LIGHTS AND SWEET MUSIC
## FOR PSYCHOLOGISTS

### A PARODY ON LOUIS MACNEICE

It's no go the country pub, it's no go by crikey,
What they want is a floor-show and a night-club called 'The
    Psyche',
Their scenery's by Sigmund Freud, their lighting by
    Lombroso,
Their dresses are by Janet and their sound effects by Charcot.

Tommy's mother bumped his head giving him a bath,
Boxed his ears until he cried, now he's a psychopath—
Thinks he sees a crocodile playing in the garden,
Puts his head between his knees and starts to pray for pardon.

It's no go Kraft-Ebbing, it's no go Dr. Jung,
They'll swear you've got 'persönlichkeitsgefühl' or
    'zweckseitzung'.

Little Lulu, quite a babe, was kissed by her Aunt Mabel,
Now she goes mad when she sees a wart-hog in its stable.
It's no go your fairy-tales, it's no go mythology,
What they want are books on sex and a treatise on psychology.

Professor Juggins kicks his wife, they say it's a neurosis;
She goes off into a trance, they tell her it's psychosis.
It's no go simplicity, it's no go love and laughter,
They'll put you under lock and key and charge you for it after.

A dervish sat beneath a palm, wrapped up in contemplation,
Freud accosted him and said, 'it's sexual sublimation!'
It's O.K. the schizophrene, it's O.K. amnesia,
But what I want's an aeroplane and a ticket for Tunisia.


Go to sleep upon your bed, lie upon your pillow,
You can switch your conscious off but you can't hold back
   your ego.
It's no go my honey-love, it's no go my poppet,
All we want is a mug of beer and a double gin to top it!

WINIFRED AMBLER


## THE SHROPSHIRE LAD

'Tis Summer Time on Bredon,
And now the farmers swear;
The cattle rise and listen
In valleys far and near,
And blush at what they hear.


But when the mists in autumn
On Bredon top are thick,
The happy hymns of farmers
Go up from fold and rick,
The cattle then are sick.

HUGH KINGSMILL

## THE LOST CHORD

Seated one day at the organ
  I jumped as if I'd been shot,
For the Dean was upon me, snarling
  'Stainer—and *make it hot.*'

All week I swung Stainer and Barnby,
  Bach, Gounod, and Bunnett in A;
I said, 'Gosh, the old bus is a wonder!'
  The Dean, with a nod, said 'Okay'.

D. B. WYNDHAM LEWIS

## TENNYSON, IN 'THE PRINCESS' WROTE: (ON SUNSET)

The splendour falls on castle walls
    And snowy summits old in story;
The long light shakes across the lakes,
    And the wild cataract leaps in glory.
Blow, bugle, blow, set the wild echoes flying,
Blow bugle; answer, echoes, dying, dying, dying.

O hark, O hear! how thin and clear,
    And thinner, clearer, farther going!
O sweet and far from cliff and scar
    The horns of Elfland faintly blowing!
Blow, let us hear the purple glens replying:
Blow bugle; answer, echoes, dying, dying, dying. . . .

## CHARLES KINGSLEY, IN 'KILLARNEY' WROTE: (ON FISHING)

Oh Mr. Froude, how wise and good
    To point us out the way to glory,
They're no great shakes, those Snowdon Lakes,
    And all their pounders myth and story.
Blow Snowdon! What's Lake Gwynant to
        Killarney,
Or spluttering Welsh to tender blarney, blarney,
    blarney?

So, Thomas Hughes, sir, if you choose,
    I'll tell you where we think of going,
To swate and far o'er cliff and scar,
    Hear horns of Elfland faintly blowing;

Blow Snowdon! There's a hundred lakes to try in,
And fresh caught salmon daily, frying, frying,
     frying.

Geology and botany
  A hundred wonders shall diskiver,
We'll flog and troll in strid and hole,
  And skim the cream of lake and river.
Blow Snowdon! Give me Ireland for my pennies;
Hurrah! for salmon, grilse, and—Dennis, Dennis,
     Dennis!

# Grave Shades from the Churchyard Gaze
# On Gay Graves that the Churchyard Shades

ARNOLD SILCOCK

*A friend of mine who helps to run a library has suggested to me that the following lines would make an apt epitaph for any librarian, so I am quoting them by way of an introduction to this chapter:*

How many decrepit, hoary, harsh, writhen, bursten-bellied, crooked, toothless, blear-eyed, impotent, rotten old men shall you see flickering still in every place. (*From Burton's 'Anatomy of Melancholy'*)

*But neither an epitaph nor a dirge need be quite so harsh and melancholy as Burton's—at least that was the opinion of the gay-spirited archbishop who wrote the following little memorializing masterpiece, the Anticipatory Dirge on Professor Buckland:*

## ANTICIPATORY DIRGE ON PROFESSOR BUCKLAND, THE GEOLOGIST

Mourn, Ammonites, mourn o'er his funeral urn,
    Whose neck we must grace no more;
Gneiss, granite, and slate—he settled your date,
    And his ye must now deplore.

[112]

Weep, caverns, weep, with infiltering drip,
   Your recesses he'll cease to explore;
For mineral veins or organic remains,
   No stratum again will he bore.

His wit shone like crystal—his knowledge profound
   From gravel to granite descended;
No trap could deceive him, no slip confound,
   No specimen, true or pretended.

Where shall we our great professor inter,
   That in peace may rest his bones?
If we hew him a rocky sepulchre,
   He'll get up and break the stones,
And examine each stratum that lies around,
For he's quite in his element underground.

If with mattock and spade his body we lay
   In the common alluvial soil;
He'll start up and snatch those tools away
   Of his own geological toil;
In a stratum so young the professor disdains
That embedded should be his organic remains.

Then exposed to the drip of some case-hardening
     spring,
   His carcass let stalactite cover;
And to Oxford the petrified sage let us bring,
   When duly encrusted all over;
There, 'mid mammoths and crocodiles, high on the
     shelf,
Let him stand as monument raised to himself.

ARCHBISHOP WHATELY

This spot is the sweetest I've seen in my life
For it raises my flowers and covers my wife.

ANON

When Sir Joshua Reynolds died
All Nature was degraded;
The King dropped a tear into the Queen's Ear,
And all his Pictures Faded.

WILLIAM BLAKE

Here Skugg lies snug
As a bug in a rug.

BENJAMIN FRANKLIN

Poor Martha Snell, she's gone away
She would if she could but she could not stay
She'd two bad legs and baddish cough
But her legs it was that carried her off.

ANON

Here lies the body of Ann Mann
Who lived an old woman
And died an old Mann.

ANON

## THE TIRED WOMAN'S EPITAPH

Here lies a poor woman who always was tired
She lived in a house where help was not hired
Her last words on earth were: 'Dear friends, I am going
Where washing ain't done, nor sweeping, nor sewing;
But everything there is exact to my wishes;
For where they don't eat there's no washing of dishes.
I'll be where loud anthems will always be ringing,
But, having no voice, I'll be clear of the singing.

[114]

Don't mourn for me now; don't mourn for me never—
I'm going to do nothing for ever and ever.'

ANON

### EPITAPH FROM ABERDEEN

Here lie the bones of Elizabeth Charlotte
Born a virgin, died a harlot
She was aye a virgin at seventeen
A remarkable thing in Aberdeen.          ANON

### IN MEMORY OF
### RICHARD COURT
who died July 31st, 1791
Aged 65 Years

My Sledge and Hammer lie Reclin'd,
My Bellows too have lost their Wind;
My Fire is out, and Forge decay'd,
And in the Dust my Vice is laid.

### ERECTED TO THE MEMORY OF
### MR. JONATHAN GILL, ESQ.
who died Febr. 6, 1751
Aged 45 Years & 6 Months

Beneath this smooth stone,
by the bone of his bone,
Sleeps Mr. Jonathan Gill,
By lies when alive this
attorney did thrive,
And now that he's dead he
lies still.

[115]

## AN EPITAPH AT GREAT TORRINGTON, DEVON

Here lies a man who was killed by lightning;
He died when his prospects seemed to be brightening.
He might have cut a flash in this world of trouble,
But the flash cut him, and he lies in the stubble.

## FROM A TOMBSTONE IN SUTTON PARISH CHURCHYARD

Here lies my poor wife,
    Without bed or blankit,
But dead as a door-nail,
    God be thankit.

## FROM A TOMBSTONE TO A FISH

that lived for twenty year, in the village of Blockley,
Gloucestershire:

In memory of the old fish Under the soil the old fish do
lie 20 year he lived and then did die He was so tame you
understand He would come and eat out of your hand Died
April the 20th 1855.

## EPITAPH FROM AUSTRALIA

God took our flower—our little Nell
He thought He too would like a smell.

ANON

## EPITAPH ON A SHREW

Here lies thank Heaven
A woman who
Quarrelled and stormed
Her whole life through
Tread lightly o'er her slumb'ring form
For fear you wake another storm.

ANON

*In 1776 the son of the parish clerk of the parish church, St.
Michael and All Angels, at Bampton, Devon, was killed outside the
church tower by a piece of ice which fell and struck him in the eye.
This much can be seen in the church records. A stone to commemorate
the tragedy, which was laid in the tower, also neglected to record the
victim's name, but it bore the following inscription:*

Bless my eyes,
Here he lies,
In a sad pickle,
Kill'd by an icicle.

## ARABELLA YOUNG

Beneath this stone
A lump of clay
Lies Arabella Young
Who on the 21st of May
1771
Began to hold her tongue.

[117]

## TO THE FOUR HUSBANDS
## OF MISS IVY SAUNDERS

### 1790, 1794, 1808, 18??

Here lies my husbands, One, Two, Three
Dumb as men could ever be
As for my Fourth, well, praise be God
He bides for a little above the sod
Alex, Ben, Sandy were the
First three names
And to make things tidy
I'll add his—James.


## FREDERICK TWITCHELL

### Departed June 11, 1811
### Aged 24 years, 5 mos.

Here lie the bones of Lazy Fred
Who wasted precious time in bed
Some plaster fell down on his head
And thanks be praised—Our
Freddie's dead.


## SOME PSEUDO-EPITAPHS

Here lies I and my three daughters
Killed by drinking Cheltenham waters.
If we'd kept to Epsom Salts
We wouldn't be lying in these 'ere vaults.

ANON

Solomon Isaacs lies in this ground.
Don't jingle money when walking around.

ANON

Here lies a Mother of Twenty-eight.
It might have been more, but now it's too late.

ANON

### EPITAPH ON HIMSELF

I was buried near this dyke,
That my friends may weep as much as they like.

WILLIAM BLAKE

### THE RASH LADY OF RYDE

There was an old lady of Ryde
Who ate some green apples, and died.
The apples (fermented inside the lamented)
Made cider inside 'er inside.

ANON

### EPITAPH ON A PARSON

Here lies the Reverend Jonathan Doe,
Where he's gone to I don't know.
If, haply to the realms above,
Farewell to happiness and love.
If, haply to a lower level,
I can't congratulate the Devil.

ANON

### LIMERICK—EPITAPH

There was an old man who averred
He had learned how to fly like a bird.

Cheered by thousands of people
He leapt from the steeple——
This tomb states the date it occurred.

ANON

## RESPIRE, ASPIRE, SUSPIRE

There was a young girl in the choir
Whose voice arose higher and higher,
  Till one Sunday night
  It rose quite out of sight,
And they found it next day on the spire.

ANON

# Premature Epitaphs

### JACOB EPSTEIN

From life's grim nightmare he is now released
Who saw in every face the lurking beast.
'A loss to Art', says friends both proud and loyal,
'A loss', say others, 'to the Café Royal.'

ANON

### LLOYD GEORGE

Count not his broken pledges as a crime:
He MEANT them, *HOW* he meant them—at the
  time.

ANON: TWENTIETH CENTURY

## MARC CONNELLY

the author of *Green Pastures*, composed this
premature epitaph for himself

Here lies Marc Connelly.
Who?

# Epigrams and Epitaphs

### AT POTTERNE, WILTS.

Here lies Mary, the wife of John Ford,
We hope her soul is gone to the Lord;
But if for Hell she has chang'd this life
She had better be there than be John Ford's wife.

### AT LEEDS

Here lies my wife,
Here lies she;
Hallelujah!
Hallelujee!

### ON DR. ISAAC LETSOME

When's people's ill they comes to I,
I physics, bleeds, and sweats 'em,
Sometimes they live, sometimes they die;
What's that to I? I Letsome.

ANON

[121]

## EPIGRAM

When Dido found Aeneas would not come,
She mourned in silence, and was Di—Do—Dum.

RICHARD PORSON

## EPITAPH
### At Upton-on-Severn

Beneath this stone in hopes of Zion
Doth lie the landlord of the Lion;
His son keeps on the business still,
Resigned unto the heavenly will.

## EPIGRAM ON THE PHRASE
### 'To Kill Time'

There's scarce a point whereon mankind agree
So well, as in their boast of killing me:
I boast of nothing, but, when I've a mind,
I think I can be even with mankind.

FROM VOLTAIRE:
DODD'S 'SELECT EPIGRAMS'

## EPITAPH ON A DYER:
## AT LINCOLN

Here lies John Hyde;
He first liv'd, and then he died;
He dyed to live, and liv'd to dye,
And hopes to live eternally.

## AN EPIGRAM–EPITAPH FOR HIS WIFE

Here lies my wife.
Here let her lie!
Now she's at rest
And so am I.

JOHN DRYDEN

## EPITAPH FOR HIMSELF

Life is jest and all things show it;
I thought so once, but now I know it.

JOHN GAY

## EPITAPH ON JOHN GAY

Well, then, poor G— lies under ground!
So there's an end of honest Jack.
So little justice here he found,
'Tis ten to one he'll ne'er come back.

ALEXANDER POPE

## JOHN BUN

Here lies John Bun,
He was killed by a gun,
His name was not Bun, but Wood,
But Wood would not rhyme with Gun,
but Bun would.

## MARY ANN

Mary Ann has gone to rest,
Safe at last on Abraham's breast,
Which may be nuts for Mary Ann
But is certainly rough on Abraham.

## A BREWER

Here lies poor Burton,
He was both hale and stout;
Death laid him on his bitter bier,
Now in another world he hops about.

## A DENTIST

Stranger! Approach this spot with gravity!
John Brown is filling his last cavity.

## JOHNNY DOW

Wha lies here?
I, Johnny Dow.
Hoo! Johnny, is that you?
Ay, man, but a'm dead now.

## ON JOHN GRUBB

When from the chrysalis of the tomb
I rise on rainbow-coloured plume
My weeping friends ye scarce will know
That I was but a Grubb below.

ANON

## ON A SCHOOLMASTER
### IN CLEISH PARISH, KINROSS-SHIRE

Here lie Willie Michie's banes;
O Satan, when ye tak him,
Gie him the schoolin' of your weans,
For clever deils he'll mak them!

ROBERT BURNS

## FROM LEYLAND CHURCHYARD, LANCASHIRE

Let the wind go free
Where'er thou be
For 'twas the wind
That kill*ed* me.

## ON MR. MUNDAY
### IN ST. OLAVE'S, SOUTHWARK, LONDON

Hallowed be the Sabbaoth
And farewell all worldly Pelfe
The Weeke begins on Tuesday
For Munday hath hang'd himselfe.

## ON THE MAKING OF A MONUMENT TO SAMUEL BUTLER IN WESTMINSTER ABBEY

While Butler, needy wretch! was still alive,
No generous patron would a dinner give:
See him, when starv'd to death and turn'd to dust,
Presented with a monumental bust!

[125]

The poet's fate is here in emblem shown,
He ask'd for bread, and he received a stone!

SAMUEL WESLEY, THE YOUNGER

## ON A CHILD OF SEVEN MONTHS OLD

If I am so quickly done for
What on earth was I begun for?

ANON

## PASSPORT TO PARADISE

He passed the bobby without any fuss,
And he passed the cart of hay,
He tried to pass a swerving bus,
And then he passed away.

ANON

## ON A HASTY WOMAN

Here lies the body of Mary Chowder,
She burst while drinking a Seidlitz Powder;
She couldn't wait till it effervesced,
So now she's gone to eternal rest.

ANON

## A HUSBAND'S EPITAPH

As I am now so you must be
Therefore prepare to follow me.

## THE WIFE'S EPITAPH

To follow you I'm not content
How do I know which way you went?

ANON

## ON A HOSIER: BY HIS HANNAH

He left his hose, his Hannah, and his love,
To sing Hosannahs in the world above.

ANON

## EPITAPH FROM A YORKSHIRE CHURCHYARD

RECOLLECTED AND WRITTEN DOWN BY HAROLD KNIGHT, R.A.

Here lies the Mother of children five
Three daughters dead two sons alive
The daughters died because they'd rather
Go to their Mother than stay with their Father.

## AN EPITAPH FROM ESSEX

Here lies the man Richard
And Mary his wife
Whose surname was Prichard
They lived without strife
And the reason was plain
They abounded in riches
They had no care nor pain
And his wife wore the breeches.

ANON

# Epitaphs from America, 17th, 18th and 19th Centuries

## A PARTHIAN SHOT

Reader, pass on!—don't waste your time
On bad biography and bitter rhyme;
For what I *am*, this cumbrous clay insures,
And what I *was*, is no affair of yours!

ANON

## POOR WOOD

Here lies one Wood
Enclosed in Wood
One Wood within another.
One of these Woods,
Is very good:
We cannot praise the other.

ANON

## THE ARTFUL DODGER

Here lies Bill Dodge
Who dodged all good
And dodged a deal of evil
But after dodging all he could
He could not dodge the Devil.

ANON

## MANNA FROM HEAVEN, NOT ANNA

The children of Israel wanted bread
The Lord he sent them manna
But this good man he wanted a wife
And the Devil sent him Anna.

ANON

# Translations from Epitaphs of Theocritus
### by C. S. CALVERLEY

*Ortho's Epitaph*

Friend, Ortho of Syracuse gives thee this charge:
Never venture out, drunk, on a wild winter's night.
I did so and died. My possessions were large;
Yet the turf that I'm clad with is strange to me quite.

*Epitaph of Cleonicus*

Man, husband existence: ne'er launch on the sea
Out of season: our tenure of life is but frail.
Think of poor Cleonicus: for Phasos sailed he
From the valleys of Syria, with many a bale:
With many a bale, ocean's tides he would stem
When the Pleiads were sinking; and he sank with them.

# Rhyming Proverbs or What Not to Do and How Not to Do It

\* \* \* \* \* \* \* \* \* \* \* \* \* \* \* \* \* \* \* \* \* \* \*

*The reason for proverbs is readily seen:*
*Thus the old and grey teach the young and green;*
*So if you are grey you can take them as read,*
*But if green they will make you see red, instead.*

ARD SLOK

## A FRENCH PROVERB ON THE SAME SUBJECT

Si jeunesse savait,
Si vieillesse pouvait.

## A MODERN PROVERB ON THE SAME SUBJECT

Teach not thy parent's mother to extract
The embryo juices of the bird by suction.
The good old lady can that feat enact
Quite irrespective of thy kind instruction.

ANON

## GAS ON THE STOMACH

What you lose of pride and dignity
You gain in comfort and benignity.

ARD SLOK

## INSPIRATION ON PERSPIRATION

Here's a little proverb you surely ought to know;
Horses sweat and men perspire but ladies only glow.

ANON

## PROVERBS FROM CHINA IN PIDGIN-ENGLISH

Supposey you one top-side man,
    No squeezey man below;
Supposey you blongey bottom-side,
    Let top-side be, galow.

One-tim in taushan wise man no talk *l*ight,
One-tim in taushan foolo shinee b*l*ight.

Who man swim best, t'hat man most gettee d*l*own;
Who *l*idee best, he most catch tumble-down.

Supposey you no make look-see for mo*ll*ow,
You ve*ll*y soon to-day make catchee so*ll*ow.

CHARLES G. LELAND

Galow: a meaningless interjection.          Taushan: a thousand.
            Light: right (*l* in italics equals 'r').

One piecee thing that my have got,
Maskee that thing my no can do.
You talkee you no sabey what?
　　Bamboo.

QUOTED BY LEWIS CARROLL

Maskee: without.


## WISDOM

Some men are wise,
And some are otherwise.

TRADITIONAL


## GRAVITY

The gravest fish is an oyster,
The gravest bird is an owl,
The gravest beast is an ass,
An' the gravest man is a fule.

SCOTS: TRADITIONAL


## CHILDREN SHOULD BE SEEN AND NOT HEARD

Speak when ye're spoken to,
Do what ye're bidden,
Come when ye're ca'd,
An' ye'll no be chidden.

SCOTS: TRADITIONAL

## HEALTH

Use three physicians' skill: first Dr. Quiet,
Then Dr. Merriman, and Dr. Diet.

TRADITIONAL

## SYMPATHY

Sympathy without relief
Is like mustard without beef.

TRADITIONAL

## FAMILIARITY BREEDS CONTEMPT

A maid often seen, a gown often worn
Are disesteemed and held in scorn.

TRADITIONAL

## HOME

A little house well filled,
A little land well tilled,
A little wife well willed.

TRADITIONAL

## THRIFT

A penny hained is a penny gained.

SCOTS: TRADITIONAL

Hained: held or saved.

## ONE GOOD TURN DESERVES ANOTHER

For one good turn another doth itch;
Claw my elbow and I'll claw thy breech.

TRADITIONAL

## FORESIGHT

Rainy days will surely come:
Take your friend's umbrella home!

MODERN: ANON

## IN PRAISE OF ALE

He that buys land buys many stones;
He that buys flesh buys many bones;
He that buys eggs buys many shells;
But he that buys good ale buys nothing else.

TRADITIONAL

## SELFISHNESS

Great spenders are bad lenders.

TRADITIONAL

## WISDOM AND FOLLY

Fools make feasts and wise men eat them;
Wise men make jests and fools repeat them.

TRADITIONAL

## ON WOMEN

Fair and foolish, black and proud,
Long and lazy, little and loud,
Fat and merry, lean and sad,
Pale and pettish, red and bad.

**TRADITIONAL**

## THE ENGLISH CLIMATE

Button to chin
Till May be in;
Cast not a clout
Till May be out.

**TRADITIONAL**

## ON CHILDREN

My son is my son till he gets him a wife,
But my daughter's my daughter for all her life.

**TRADITIONAL**

If wishes were horses beggars wad ride
And a' the warld be drowned in pride.

**SCOTS: TRADITIONAL**

Idle bodies are busybodies.

**TRADITIONAL**

## DIPLOMACY

He that would the daughter win,
Must with the mother first begin.

**TRADITIONAL**

## ON POVERTY

La pauvreté n'est pas un péché;
Mieux vaut cependant la cacher!

FRENCH: TRADITIONAL

*Poverty is no crime—all the same it is better to hide it!*

## ON LOVE

Follow love and it will flee, flee love and it will follow thee.

TRADITIONAL

## DISCRETION

'Softly, softly',
Catchee monkey.

NEGRO: TRADITIONAL

## SUCCESS

Cheek and chawl
Does it all.

MIDLANDS: TRADITIONAL

*An interpretation of this is: 'cheek' (self-assurance) and 'chawl'*
*(jowl—i.e. a strong jaw, or 'grit') accomplishes everything.*

# Come Live With Me and Be My Love

\* \* \* \* \* \* \* \* \* \* \* \* \* \* \* \* \* \* \* \* \* \* \*

A POEM WRITTEN AFTER SWIMMING THE HELLESPONT

*Lord Byron, on the 3rd of May 1810, accompanied by Lieutenant Ekenhead of the frigate* Salsette, *then lying at anchor in the Dardanelles, swam 'the Hellespont', from Abydos to Sestos. Later Lord Byron wrote the following account of this feat, to which he had been inspired by the famous story of Hero and Leander:*

'*The whole distance from the place whence we started to our landing on the other side, including the length we were carried by the current, was computed by those on board the frigate at upwards of four English miles; though the actual breadth is barely one. The rapidity of the current is such that no boat can row directly across, and it may, in some measure, be estimated from the circumstance of the whole distance being accomplished by one of the parties in an hour and five, and by the other in an hour and ten minutes. The water was extremely cold, from the melting of the mountain snows. About three weeks before, in April, we had made an attempt; but having ridden all the way from the Troad the same morning, and the water being of an icy chillness, we found it necessary to postpone the completion till the frigate anchored below the castles, when we swam the straits, as just stated, entering a considerable way above the European, and landing below the Asiatic fort. Chevalier says that a young Jew swam the same distance for his mistress; and Oliver mentions its having been done by a Neapolitan; but our consul, Tarragone, remembered neither of these circumstances, and tried to dissuade us from the attempt. A number of the* Salsette's *crew were known to have accomplished a greater distance; and the only thing that surprised me was, that, as doubts had been entertained of the truth of Leander's story, no traveller had ever endeavoured to ascertain its practicability.'*

If, in the month of dark December,
　　Leander, who was nightly wont
(What maid will not the tale remember?)
　　To cross thy stream, broad Hellespont!

If, when the wintry tempest roar'd,
　　He sped to Hero, nothing loath,
And thus of old thy current pour'd,
　　Fair Venus! how I pity both!

For *me*, degenerate modern wretch,
　　Though in the genial month of May
My dripping limbs I faintly stretch,
　　And think I've done a feat to-day,

But since he cross'd the rapid tide,
　　According to the doubtful story,
To woo—and—Lord knows what beside,
　　And swam for Love, as I for Glory,

'Twere hard to say who fared the best:
　　Sad mortals! thus the Gods still plague you!
He lost his labour, I my jest;
　　For he was drown'd, and I've the ague.

LORD BYRON

## THE BALLAD OF THE OYSTERMAN

It was a tall young oysterman lived by the river-side,
His shop was just upon the bank, his boat was on the tide;
The daughter of a fisherman, that was so straight and slim,
Lived over on the other bank, right opposite to him.

It was the pensive oysterman that saw a lovely maid,
Upon a moonlight evening, a sitting in the shade;
He saw her wave her handkerchief, as much as if to say,
'I'm wide awake, young oysterman, and all the folks away'.

Then up arose the oysterman, and to himself said he,
'I guess I'll leave the skiff at home, for fear that folks should
    see;
I read it in the story-book, that, for to kiss his dear,
Leander swam the Hellespont—and I will swim this here.'

And he has leaped into the waves, and crossed the shining
    stream,
And he has clambered up the bank, all in the moonlight gleam;
O there were kisses sweet as dew, and words as soft as rain—
But they have heard her father's step, and in he leaps again!

Out spoke the ancient fisherman—'O what was that my
    daughter?'
' 'Twas nothing but a pebble, sir, I threw into the water.'
'And what is that, pray tell me, love, that paddles off so fast?'
'It's nothing but a porpoise, sir, that's been a swimming past.'

Out spoke the ancient fisherman—'Now bring me my har-
    poon!
I'll get into my fishing-boat, and fix the fellow soon.'

Down fell that pretty innocent, as falls a snow-white lamb,
Her hair drooped round her pallid cheeks, like seaweed on a
   clam.

Alas for those two loving ones! she waked not from her
   swound,
And he was taken with cramp, and in the waves was drowned;
But Fate has metamorphosed them, in pity of their woe,
And now they keep an oyster-shop for mermaids down below.

OLIVER WENDELL HOLMES

## THE LADY WITH TECHNIQUE

As I was letting down my hair
I met a guy who didn't care;
He didn't care again to-day—
I *love* 'em when they get that way!

HUGHES MEARNS

## THE KISS

'I saw you take his kiss!' ''Tis true'.
'O, modesty!' ''Twas strictly kept:
He thought me asleep: at least, I knew
He thought I thought he thought I slept.'

COVENTRY PATMORE

## WHAT MY LOVER SAID

By the merest chance in the twilight gloom,
   In the orchard path he met me;
In the tall, wet grass, with its faint perfume,
And I tried to pass, but he made no room,

[140]

Oh, I tried, but he would not let me.
So I stood and blushed till the grass grew red,
  With my face bent down above it,
While he took my hand as he whispering said—
(How the clover lifted each pink, sweet head,
To listen to all that my lover said;
  Oh, the clover in bloom, I love it!)


I am sure that he knew when he held me fast,
  That I must be all unwilling;
For I tried to go, and I would have passed,
As the night was come with its dew, at last,
  And the sky with its stars was filling.
But he clasped me close when I would have fled,
  And he made me hear his story,
And his soul came out from his lips and said:
(How the stars crept out where the white moon led
To listen to all that my lover said:
  Oh, the moon and the stars in glory!)

HOMER GREENE

*From the 'New York Evening Post', 1875*


## TIME LOST IN WOOING

The time I've lost in wooing,
  In watching and pursuing
    The light that lies
    In woman's eyes,
Has been my heart's undoing.
Though wisdom oft has sought me,

I scorn'd the lore she brought me.
　My only books
　Were woman's looks,
And folly's all they've taught me!

THOMAS MOORE

Lines from

## THE EMPEROR OF THE MOON

All soft and sweet the maid appears,
　With looks that know no art,
And though she yields with trembling fears,
　She yields with all her heart.

APHRA BEHN (*née* AMIS): 1640–89

## FROM THE 'PASTORALS'

But see, the shepherds shun the noon-day heat,
The lowing herds to murm'ring brooks retreat,
To closer shades the panting flocks remove;
Ye Gods! and is there no relief for love?

ALEXANDER POPE

## A WEDDING

I tell thee, Dick, where I have been;
Where I the rarest things have seen;
　Oh, things without compare!
Such sights again can not be found
In any place on English ground,
　Be it at wake or fair.

At Charing Cross, hard by the way
Where we (thou know'st) do sell our hay,[1]
    There is a house with stairs;
And there did I see coming down
Such folks as are not in our town;
    Vorty at least, in pairs.

Amongst the rest one pest'lent fine
(His beard no bigger tho' than thine)
    Walk'd on before the rest;
Our landlord looks like nothing to him;
The King (God bless him!) 'twould undo him,
    Should he go still so drest.

But wot you want? The youth was going
To make an end of all his woing;
    The parson for him staid:
Yet by his leave, for all his haste,
He did not so much wish all past,
    Perchance as did the maid.

The maid (and thereby hangs a tale)
For such a maid no Whitson-ale
    Could ever yet produce;
No grape that's kindly ripe, could be
So round, so plump, so soft, as she
    Nor half so full of juyce.

Her feet beneath her petticoat,
Like little mice, stole in and out,
    As if they fear'd the light:

---

[1] The Haymarket.

But oh! she dances such a way;
No sun upon an Easter day
   Is half so fine a sight.[1]

Her cheeks so rare, a white was on,
No daisie makes comparison
   (Who sees them is undone);
For streaks of red were mingled there,
Such as are on a Cath'rine pear,
   The side that's next the Sun.

Just in the nick the Cook knock'd thrice,
And all the waiters in a trice
   His summons did obey;
Each serving man, with dish in hand,
March'd boldly up like our train'd band,
   Presented, and away.

When all the meat was on the table,
What man of knife, or teeth, was able
   To stay to be entreated?
And this the very reason was,
Before the parson could say grace
   The company was seated.

Now hats fly off, and youths carouse;
Healths first go round, and then the house,
   The bride's came thick and thick;
And when 'twas named another's health,
Perhaps he made it hers by stealth,
   (And who could help it. Dick?)

---

[1] There was a jolly legend that the sun would dance on Easter day.

O' th' sudden, up they rise and dance;
Then sit again, and sigh, and glance:
   Then dance again, and kiss:
Thus sev'ral ways the time did pass,
Till ev'ry woman wish'd her place
   And ev'ry man wish'd his.

By this time all were stol'n aside
To counsel and undress the bride;
   But that he must not know:
And yet 'twas thought he guest her mind,
And did not mean to stay behind
   Above an hour or so.

**SIR JOHN SUCKLING: SEVENTEENTH CENTURY**

## WHOLLY MATRIMONY

He was rich and old and she
Was thirty-two or thirty-three.
She gave him fifteen years to live—
The only thing she meant to give.

**JUSTIN RICHARDSON**

## SISTERS

If only I hadn't had sisters
How much more romantic I'd be
But my sisters were such little blisters
That all women are sisters to me.

**JUSTIN RICHARDSON**

*From the series 'Wholly Matrimony'.* The Tatler.

### SISTERS-IN-LAW

They look'd so alike as they sat at their work,
(What a pity it is that one isn't a Turk!)
The same glances and smiles, the same habits and arts,
The same tastes, the same frocks, and (no doubt) the
    same hearts.
The same irresistible cut of their jibs,
The same little jokes, and the same little fibs—
That I thought the best way to get out of my pain
Was by—*heads* for Maria, and *woman* for Jane;
For hang *me* if it seem'd it could matter a straw,
Which dear became wife, and which sister-in-law.

But now, I will own, I feel rather inclined
To suspect I've some reason to alter my mind;
And the doubt in my breast daily grows a more strong
    one,
That they're not *quite* alike, and I've taken the wrong
    one.
Jane is always so gentle, obliging, and cool;
Never calls me a monster—not even a fool;
All our little contentions, 'tis she makes them up,
And she knows how much sugar to put in my cup:
Yes, I sometimes *have* wish'd—Heav'n forgive me the
    flaw!—
That my very dear wife was my sister-in-law.

Oh, your sister-in-law is a dangerous thing!
The daily comparisons, too, she will bring!
Wife—curl-paper'd, slip-shod, unwash'd and undress'd;
She—ringleted, booted, and 'fix'd' in her best;

Wife—sulky, or storming, or preaching, or prating;
She—merrily singing, or laughing, or chatting:
Then the innocent freedom her friendship allows
To the happy half-way between mother and spouse.
In short, if the Devil e'er needs a cat's paw,
He can't find one more sure than a sister-in-law.

That no good upon earth can be had undiluted
Is a maxim experience has seldom refuted;
And preachers and poets have proved it is so
With abundance of tropes, more or less *apropos*.
Every light has its shade, every rose has its thorn,
The cup has its headache, its poppy the corn;
There's a fly in the ointment, a spot on the sun—
In short, they've used all illustrations—but one;
And have left it to me the most striking to draw—
Viz. that none, without *wives*, can have *sisters-in-law*.

ANON (ABOUT 1850)

## WINE, WOMEN AND WEDDING

The glances over cocktails
That seemed to be so sweet
Don't seem quite so amorous
Over the Shredded Wheat.

ANON

## BUT A MARGIN

The difference between
Butter and margar*ine*
Is the distant connection
Between love and affection.

If this be error and upon me proved
I cannot taste, nor no man ever loved.

*By an anonymous writer in the*
*Evening Standard's Londoner's Diary.*

## CASTAWAY

He grabbed me round my slender neck,
I could not shout or scream,
He carried me into his room
Where we could not be seen;
He tore away my flimsy wrap
And gazed upon my form—
I was so cold and still and damp,
While he was wet and warm.
His feverish mouth he pressed to mine—
I let him have his way—
He drained me of my very self,
I could not say him nay.
He made me what I am. Alas!
That's why you find me here . . .
A broken vessel—broken glass—
That once held Bottled Beer.

**ANON**

## COMRADES IN ARMS
## CONVERSATION PIECE

'Bon soir, ma chérie,
Comment allez-vous?'
'Je suis très bien,
Merci beaucoup.'

'Etes-vous fiancé?'
'San fairy-ann.'
'Voulez-vous promenader avec moi ce soir?'
'Oui, oui——'
'Combien?'

**ANON**

## FATAL LOVE

Poor Hal caught his death standing under a spout,
Expecting till midnight when Nan would come out,
But fatal his patience, as cruel the dame,
And curs'd was the weather that quench'd the man's flame.

Whoe'er thou art, that read'st these moral lines,
Make love at home, and go to bed betimes.

MATTHEW PRIOR: 1664–1721

## SYMPATHY

A knight and a lady once met in a grove,
While each was in quest of a fugitive love;
A river ran mournfully murmuring by,
And they wept in its waters for sympathy.

'Oh, never was knight such a sorrow that bore!'
'Oh, never was maid so deserted before!'
'From life and its woes let us instantly fly,
And jump in together for company!'

They search'd for an eddy that suited the deed,
But here was a bramble and there was a weed;

[149]

'How tiresome it is!' said the fair with a sigh;
So they sat down to rest them in company.

They gazed at each other, the maid and the knight;
How fair was her form, and how goodly his height!
'One mournful embrace,' sobb'd the youth, 'ere we die!'
So kissing and crying kept company.

'Oh, had I but loved such an angel as you!'
'Oh, had but my swain been a quarter as true!'
'To miss such perfection how blinded was I!'
Sure now they were excellent company!

At length spoke the lass, 'twixt a smile and a tear,
'The weather is cold for a watery bier;
When summer returns we may easily die—
Till then let us sorrow in company!'

REGINALD HEBER

Lines from

A RONDEAU ON BLACK EYES

By two black eyes my heart was won,
Sure never wretch was more undone.
To Celia with my suit I came,
    But she, regardless of her prize,
Thought proper to reward my flame
    With two black eyes!

ANON

## AN EXPOSTULATION

When late I attempted your pity to move,
   What made you so deaf to my prayers?
Perhaps it was right to dissemble your love,
   But—why did you kick me downstairs?

               ISAAC BICKERSTAFFE

## THE FEMALE FRIEND

In this imperfect, gloomy scene
   Of complicated ill,
How rarely is a day serene,
   The throbbing bosom still!
Will not a beauteous landscape bright
   Or music's soothing sound,
Console the heart, afford delight,
   And throw sweet peace around?
They may; but never comfort lend
Like an accomplish'd female friend!

With such a friend the social hour
   In sweetest pleasure glides;
There is in female charms a power
   Which lastingly abides:
The fragrance of the blushing rose,
   Its tints and splendid hue,
Will with the season decompose,
   And pass as flitting dew;
On firmer ties his joys depend
Who has a faithful female friend!

As orbs revolve, and years recede
    And seasons onward roll,
The fancy may on beauties feed
    With discontented soul;
A thousand objects bright and fair
    May for a moment shine,
Yet many a sigh and many a tear
    But mark their swift decline;
While lasting joys the man attend
Who has a polish'd female friend!

REV. CORNELIUS WHUR: 1782–1853

## THE ANGEL AND THE THIEF

I asked a Thief to steal me a peach
He turned up his eyes.
I asked a lithe lady to lie her down
'Holy and Meek' she cries.

As soon as I went an Angel came.
He winked at the Thief and smiled at
    the dame.

And without one word spoke
Had a peach from the tree
And 'twixt earnest and jest
Enjoyed the lady.

WILLIAM BLAKE: 1757–1827

## MARRIAGE MARKET

These panting damsels, dancing for their lives,
Are only maidens waltzing into wives.
Those smiling matrons are appraisers sly,
Who regulate the dance, the squeeze, the sigh,
And each base cheapening buyer having chid,
Knock down their daughters to the noblest bid!

ANON (EIGHTEENTH CENTURY)

## EPIGRAM

That which doth make this life delightful prove
Is a genteel sufficiency—and love!

ANON (SEVENTEENTH CENTURY)

## A LEAP-YEAR EPISODE

Can I forget that winter night
   In eighteen eighty-four,
When Nellie, charming little sprite,
   Came tapping at the door?
'Good evening, miss,' I blushing said,
   For in my heart I knew—
And, knowing, hung my pretty head—
   That Nellie came to woo.

She clasped my big, red hand, and fell
   Adown upon her knees,
And cried: 'You know I love you well,
   So be my husband, please!'
And then she swore she'd ever be
   A tender wife and true—
Ah, what delight it was to me
   That Nellie came to woo!

She'd lace my shoes and darn my hose
   And mend my shirts, she said;
And grease my comely Roman nose
   Each night on going to bed;
She'd build the fires and fetch the coal,
   And split the kindling, too—
Love's perjuries o'erwhelmed her soul
   When Nellie came to woo.

And as I, blushing, gave no check
   To her advances rash,
She twined her arms about my neck,
   And toyed with my moustache;

[154]

And then she pleaded for a kiss,
    While I—what could I do
But coyly yield me to that bliss
    When Nellie came to woo?

I am engaged, and proudly wear
    A gorgeous diamond ring,
And I shall wed my lover fair
    Some time in gentle spring.
I face my doom without a sigh—
    And so, forsooth, would you,
If you but loved as fond as I
    The Nellie who came to woo.
        ATTRIBUTED TO EUGENE FIELD: 1850–95

## TWO VALENTINES

*(I) Lines Suggested by the Fourteenth of February*
    Darkness succeeds to twilight:
        Through lattice and through skylight,
    The stars no doubt, if one looked out,
        Might be observed to shine:
    And sitting by the embers
        I elevate my members
    On a stray chair, and then and there
        Commence a Valentine.
                C. S. CALVERLEY

*(II) Lines Suggested by the Fourteenth of February*
    Ere the morn the East has crimsoned,
        When the stars are twinkling there,
    (As they did in Watt's Hymns, and
        Made him wonder what they were:)
           [155]

When the forest-nymphs are beading
    Fern and flower with silvery dew—
My infallible proceeding
    Is to wake, and think of you.

When the hunter's ringing bugle
    Sounds farewell to field and copse,
And I sit before my frugal
    Meal of gravy-soup and chops:
When (as Gray remarks) 'the moping
    Owl doth to the moon complain,'
And the hour suggests eloping—
    Fly my thoughts to you again.

May my dreams be granted never?
    Must I aye endure affliction
Rarely realized, if ever
    In our wildest works of fiction?
Madly Romeo loved his Juliet;
    Copperfield began to pine
When he hadn't been to school yet—
    But their loves were cold to mine.

Give me hope, the least, the dimmest,
    Ere I drain the poisoned cup:
Tell me I may tell the chymist
    Not to make that arsenic up!
Else the heart must cease to throb in
    This my breast; and when, in tones
Hushed, men ask: 'Who killed Cock Robin?'
    They'll be told: 'Miss Clara J——s.'

C. S. CALVERLEY

Lines from
## NOTHING TO WEAR

I should mention just here, that out of Miss Flora's
Two hundred and fifty or sixty adorers,
I had just been selected as he who should throw all
The rest in the shade, by the gracious bestowal
   On myself, after twenty or thirty rejections,
   Of those fossil remains which she called 'her
     affections',
   And that rather decay'd, but well-known work of
     art,
   Which Miss Flora persisted in styling 'her heart'.
   So we were engaged. Our troth had been plighted,
   Not by moonbeam or starbeam, by fountain or grove,
   But in a front parlour, most brilliantly lighted,
   Beneath the gas fixtures we whisper'd our love.
   Without any romance, or raptures, or sighs,
   Without any tears in Miss Flora's blue eyes;
   Or blushes, or transports, or such silly actions,
   It was one of the quietest business transactions;
   With a very small sprinkling of sentiment, if any,
   And a very large diamond imported by Tiffany.
                   WILLIAM ALLAN BUTLER


## THE PLAYBOY OF THE DEMI-WORLD:
### 1938

   Aloft in Heavenly Mansions, Doubleyou One—
   Just Mayfair flats, but certainly sublime—
   You'll find the abode of D'Arcy Honeybunn,
   A rose-red sissy half as old as time.

Peace cannot age him, and no war could kill
The genial tenant of those cosy rooms,
He's lived there always and he lives there still,
Perennial pansy, hardiest of blooms.

There you'll encounter aunts of either sex,
Their jokes equivocal or over-ripe,
Ambiguous couples wearing slacks and specs
And the stout Lesbian knocking out her pipe.

The rooms are crammed with flowers and *objets d'art*,
A Ganymede still hands the drinks—and plenty!
D'Arcy still keeps a rakish-looking car
And still behaves the way he did at twenty.

A ruby pin is fastened in his tie,
The scent he uses is *Adieu Sagesse*,
His shoes are suede, and as the years go by
His tailor's bill's not getting any less.

He cannot whistle, always rises late,
Is good at indoor sports and parlour-tricks,
Mauve is his favourite colour, and his gait
Suggests a peahen walking on hot bricks.

He prances forward with his hands outspread
And folds all comers in a gay embrace,
A wavy toupee on his hairless head,
A fixed smile on his often-lifted face.

'My dear!' he lisps, to whom all men are dear,
'How perfectly enchanting of you!' turns

[158]

Towards his guests and twitters, 'Look who's here!
Do come and help us fiddle while Rome burns!'

'The kindest man alive,' so people say,
  'Perpetual youth!' But have you seen his eyes?
The eyes of some old saurian in decay
That asks no questions and is told no lies.

Under the fribble lurks a worn-out sage
Heavy with disillusion, and alone;
So never say to D'Arcy, 'Be your age!'—
He'd shrivel up at once or turn to stone.

**WILLIAM PLOMER**

## EPITHALAMIUM

Oh, what a wedding of beauty and brains—
The fair Lopokova, and John Maynard Keynes!

## PRAYER TO ST. CATHERINE

St. Catherine, St. Catherine, O lend me thine aid,
  And grant that I never may die an old maid.

A husband, St. Catherine,
A *good* one, St. Catherine;
But arn-a-one better than
Narn-a-one, St. Catherine.

Sweet St. Catherine,
A husband, St. Catherine,

Handsome, St. Catherine,
Rich, St. Catherine,
*Soon*, St. Catherine.*

TRADITIONAL (HAMPSHIRE)

## THE * ITSELF HAS A HISTORY: LISTEN:

An author owned an asterisk
And kept it in his den
Where he wrote tales which had large
  sales
Of erring maids and men,
And always, when he reached the point
Where carping censors lurk,
He called upon the asterisk
To do his dirty work!

ANON

(CANADIAN 'GOOD HOUSEKEEPING')

*A Verse composed by Sweet Seventeen, about the Famous Joint
Headmistresses of the Victorian Seminary for Young Ladies—
Cheltenham College.*

Miss Buss and Miss Beale
Cupid's darts do not feel;
Oh, how different from us
Are Miss Beale and Miss Buss.

ANON

---

* A well-known guide-book says of Milton in Hampshire that there is a
chapel there, which, as is often the case with hilltop churches, is dedicated to
St. Catherine of Alexandria, whose body is said to have been buried by angels
on Mount Sinai. St. Catherine is the patron saint of spinsters, her day still being celebrated by the midinettes of Paris. The rhymes were in use in Milton
within living memory.

## JIG FOR SACKBUTS
*On Perceiving a Fresh Outbreak of Folkdancing in Essex.*

Taborer beat
   Your little drum;
Things are looking
   Decidedly rum

To poor Mr. Merrythought,
   Dancing apart;
Bells on his trousers,
   Hell in his heart

Since round the Maypole
   Frolics Miss Prism,
Plainly not knowing
   Its symbolism.

TIMOTHY SHY
IN THE 'NEWS CHRONICLE'

# Cats and Dogs with Feral Features: also all other Kinds of Creatures

\* \* \* \* \* \* \* \* \* \* \* \* \* \* \* \* \* \* \* \* \* \* \* \*

*Cats: Let me introduce—noisy, when on the loose.*
*Dogs too: whenever they, sauntering upon their way, spot*
*pussy on the loose, wait not to introduce, gently, the*
*subject 'chase'; but set a 'killing' pace. . . .*
*I—following their lead—here say 'who runs may read'.*

### ST. JEROME AND HIS LION

St. Jerome in his study kept a great big cat,
It's always in his pictures, with its feet upon the mat.
Did he give it milk to drink, in a little dish?
When it came to Fridays, did he give it fish?
If I lost my little cat, I'd be sad without it;
I should ask St. Jeremy what to do about it;
I should ask St. Jeremy, just because of that,
For he's the only saint I know who kept a pussy cat.

ANON

### Lines from
### SAD MEMORIES

They tell me I am beautiful: they praise my silken hair,
My little feet that silently slip on from stair to stair:
They praise my pretty trustful face and innocent grey eye;
Fond hands caress me oftentimes, yet would that I might die!

Why was I born to be abhorr'd of man and bird and beast?
The bullfinch marks me stealing by, and straight his song hath
 ceased;
The shrewmouse eyes me shudderingly, then flees; and, worse
 than that,
The housedog he flees after me—why was I born a cat?

Men prize the heartless hound who quits dry-eyed his native
 land;
Who wags a mercenary tail and licks a tyrant hand.
The leal true cat they prize not, that if e'er compell'd to roam
Still flies, when let out of the bag, precipitately home.

They call me cruel. Do I know if mouse or song-bird feels?
I only know they make me light and salutary meals:
And if, as 'tis my nature to, ere I devour I tease 'em,
 Why should a low-bred gardener's boy pursue me with a
 besom?

Should china fall or chandeliers, or anything but stocks—
Nay stocks, when they're in flowerpots—the cat expects hard
 knocks:
 Should ever anything be missed—milk, coals, umbrellas,
 brandy—
The cat's pitched into with a boot or anything that's handy....

C. S. CALVERLEY

## A CAT'S CONSCIENCE

A Dog will often steal a bone,
But conscience lets him not alone,
And by his tail his guilt is known.

[163]

But cats consider theft a game,
And, howsoever you may blame,
Refuse the slightest sign of shame.

When food mysteriously goes,
The chances are that Pussy knows
More than she leads you to suppose.

And hence there is no need for you,
If Puss declines a meal or two,
To feel her pulse and make ado.

ANON

## THERE WAS A YOUNG CURATE OF KEW

There was a young curate of Kew,
Who kept a Tom cat in a pew;
   He taught it to speak
   Alphabetical Greek,
But it never got further than $\mu$.

Said the curate, 'Dear Pussy, you know,
Is that really as far as you go?
   If you only would try,
   You might get up to $\pi$,
Or even $\upsilon$ or $\rho$.'

ANON

## THE POET AND THE FLY

*A few lines from this long Poem*

'Fly! Thy brisk unmeaning buzz
Would have roused the man of Uz;

And besides thy buzzing, I
Fancy thou'rt a stinging fly.
Fly—who'rt peering, I am certain,
At me now from yonder curtain;
Busy, curious, thirsty fly
(As thou'rt clept, I well know why)—
Cease, if only for a single
Hour, to make my being tingle!
Flee to some loved haunt of thine;
To the valleys where the kine,
Udder-deep in grasses cool,
Or the rushy-margined pool,
Strive to lash thy murmurous kin
(Vainly) from their dappled skin!
Round the steed's broad nostrils flit,
Till he foams and champs the bit,
And, reluctant to be bled,
Tosses high his lordly head.
I have seen a thing no larger
Than thyself assail a charger;
He—who unconcerned would stand
All the braying of the band,
Who disdained trombone and drum—
Quailed before that little hum.
I have seen one flaunt his feelers
'Fore the steadiest of wheelers,
And at once the beast would bound,
Kangaroo-like, off the ground.
Lithe o'er moor and marish hie,
Like thy king, the Dragon-fly;
With the burnished bee skim over
Sunlit uplands white with clover;
Or, low-brooding on the lea,

Warn the swain of storms to be!
—Need I tell thee how to act?
Do just anything in fact.
Haunt my cream ('twill make thee plump).
Filch my sugar, every lump;
Round my matin-coat keep dodging,
In my necktie find a lodging
(Only, now that I reflect, I
Rather seldom wear a necktie);
Perforate my Sunday hat;
(It's a new one—what of that?)
Honeycomb my cheese, my favourite,
Thy researches will but flavour it;
Spoil my dinner-beer, and sneak up
Basely to my evening tea-cup;
Palter with my final toddy;
But respect my face and body!
Hadst thou been a painted hornet,
Or a wasp, I might have borne it;
But a common fly or gnat!
Come, my friend, get out of that.'

Dancing down, the insect here
Stung him smartly on the ear;
For a while—like some cheap earring—
Clung there, then retreated jeering.
(As men jeer, in prose or rhyme,
So may flies, in pantomime;
We discern not in their buzz
Language, but the poet does.) . . .

C. S. CALVERLEY

the honey bee

the honey bee is sad and cross
and wicked as a weasel
and when she perches on you boss
she leaves a little measle.

DON MARQUIS

## THE WASP

A severed wasp yet drank the juice
Of a ripe pear upon a plate,
And one did idly meditate
What was the use.

Yet round about us, spent and done,
With hands already growing cold,
We see half-men still scraping gold,
Its uses gone.

EDEN PHILLPOTTS

## THE HORNET

A 'ornet lived in an 'oller tree
A narsty spiteful twud were 'e.

TRADITIONAL: SOMERSET

Twud: toad

## EVOLUTION

When we were a soft amoeba, in ages past and gone,
Ere you were Queen of Sheba, or I King Solomon,

[167]

Alone and undivided, we lived a life of sloth,
Whatever you did, I did; one dinner served for both.
Anon came separation, by fission and divorce,
A lonely pseudopodium I wandered on my course.

*Published anonymously in 'Life',*
*by* SIR ARTHUR SHIPLEY, *allegedly*

## THE CORMORANT

The common cormorant or shag
Lays eggs inside a paper bag,
The reason you will see no doubt—
It is to keep the lightning out.
But what these unobservant birds
Have never noticed is that herds
Of wandering bears may come with buns
And steal the bags to hold the crumbs.

ANON

## THE RABBIT

The rabbit has a charming face:
Its private life is a disgrace.
I really dare not name to you
The awful things that rabbits do;
Things that your paper never prints—
You only mention them in hints.
They have such lost, degraded souls
No wonder they inhabit holes;
When such depravity is found
It only can live underground.

IN PART ANON AND PARTLY
BY NAOMI ROYDE SMITH

## BALLAD OF THE FOXES

There is a golden glory in my song
As of a picture by Carpaccio,
For it is of the early morning-time
When every man believed with tender faith
That animals could talk—oh lovely lore!
So, lady, listen as the lay runs on.

There was a goose, and she was travelling
Across the land for her dyspepsia,
And at the noontide sat to rest herself
In a small thicket, when there came along
Two starving foxes, perishing to find
Something which was not too-too-utter-ish
To serve for dinner. And as they were wild
For want of food, it was but natural
That they should likewise be confounded cross;
Oh, lady, listen as the lay runs on!

And as they halted near the thicket, one
Of them observed, 'If you were half as sharp
As books make out, you would not now, I'll bet,
Be ravenous enough to gnaw the grass.'
'And if you were as big, or half as big,
As you believe you are,' snarled Number Two,
'You'd be a lion of the largest size
*Minus* his roar, and pluck, and dignity.'
Oh, listen, lady, as the lay runs on!

'Please to observe I want no impudence
From any fifteen-nickel quadruped
Of your peculiar shape', snapped Number One.

'And if you give me but another note
Of your chin-music,' snarled out Number Two,
'I'll make a wreck of you, you wretched beast,
Beyond insurance—bet your tail on that!'
Oh, lady, listen as the lay runs on!

'You are the champion of all the beasts!'
'And you the upper scum of all the frauds.'
'You are the weathercock of infamy.'
'And you the lightning-rod of falsehood's spire.'
'You are a thief!' 'Ditto.' 'You lie.' 'I ain't.'
'Shut up, you goy!' And hearing this, the goose
Could bear no more, but walking from the bush,
Put on expression most benevolent,
And said, 'Oh, gentlemen, for shame! for shame!
I'll settle this dispute: in the first place
Let me remark, as an impartial friend——'
Oh listen, lady, as the lay runs on!

But she did not remark, because they made
A rush at her and caught her by the throat,
And ate her up; and as they picked their teeth
With toothpicks made of her last pin-feathers,
The first observed, and that quite affably,
'Only a goose would ever make attempt
To settle a dispute when foxes fight'—
Oh, lady, listen as the lay runs on!

'And while I have a very great respect
For any peacemaker,' said Number Two,
'I would suggest that I invariably
Have found, if they be really honest folk
Who interfere with reprobates like us,

[170]

They're always eaten up; there is, I think,
More clanship between devils any day
Than among all the angels. Interest
Binds us together, and howe'er we fight
Among ourselves to ease our bitter blood,
We do not hate each other half as much
As we do hate the good. Neighbours who fight
Can generally take most perfect care,
Not only of themselves, but of the goose
Who sticks her bill into the fuss they make.
This banquet now adjourns until it meets
Another winged angel of the sort
Which it has just discussed—may it be soon!'
Lady, this lyric runs no further on.

CHARLES G. LELAND

## DOCTOR LOBSTER

A Perch, who had the toothache, once
Thus moan'd, like any human dunce:
'Why must great souls exhaust so soon
Life's thin and unsubstantial boon?
Existence on such sculpin terms—
Their vulgar loves and hard-won worms—
What is it all but dross to me,
Whose nature craves a larger sea;
Whose inches, six from head to tail,
Enclose the spirit of a whale;
Who, if great baits were still to win,
By watchful eye and fearless fin
Might with the Zodiac's awful twain
Room for a third immortal gain?

[171]

Better the crowd's unthinking plan—
The hook, the jerk, the frying-pan!
O Death, thou ever roaming shark,
Ingulf me in eternal dark!'

The speech was cut in two by flight:
A real shark had come in sight;
No metaphoric monster, one
It soothes despair to call upon,
But stealthy, sidelong, grim, I wis,
A bit of downright Nemesis;
While it recovered from the shock,
Our fish took shelter 'neath a rock:
This was an ancient lobster's house,
A lobster of prodigious *nous*,
So old that barnacles had spread
Their white encampments o'er its head—
And of experience so stupend,
His claws were blunted at the end,
Turning life's iron pages o'er,
That shut and can be oped no more.

Stretching a hospitable claw,
'At once,' said he, 'the point I saw;
My dear young friend, your case I rue,
Your great-great-grandfather I knew;
He was a tried and tender friend
I know—I ate him in the end!
In this vile sea a pilgrim long,
Still my sight's good, my memory strong;
The only sign that age is near
Is a slight deafness in this ear;
I understand your case as well

As this my old familiar shell;
This sorrow's a new-fangled notion,
Come in since first I knew the ocean;
We had no radicals, nor crimes,
Nor lobster-pots, in good old times;
Your traps and nets and hooks we owe
To Messieurs Louis Blanc and Co.;
I say to all my sons and daughters,
Shun Red Republican hot waters;
No lobster ever cast his lot
Among the reds, but went to pot:
Your trouble's in the jaw, you said?
Come, let me just nip off your head,
And, when a new one comes, the pain
Will never trouble you again:
Nay, nay, fear naught: 'tis nature's law;
Four times I've lost this starboard claw;
And still, ere long, another grew,
Good as the old—and better too!'

The perch consented, and next day
An osprey, marketing that way,
Picked up a fish without a head,
Floating with belly up, stone dead.

### MORAL

Sharp are the teeth of ancient saws,
And sauce for goose is gander's sauce;
But perch's heads aren't lobster's claws.

JAMES RUSSELL LOWELL

## THE HARE AND THE TORTOISE
### MODERN VERSION

A.rabbit raced a turtle,
You know the turtle won;
And Mister Bunny came in late,
A little hot cross bun!

*From the Song in Hill-Billy Album No. 1.*
*'It Ain't Gonna Rain No Mo'' by Francis Day*
*and Hunter.*


## A FISH STORY

A whale of great porosity
And small specific gravity,
Dived down with much velocity
Beneath the sea's concavity.

But soon the weight of water
Squeezed in his fat immensity,
Which varied—as it ought to—
Inversely as his density.

It would have moved to pity
An Ogre or a Hessian,
To see poor Spermaceti
Thus suffering compression.

The while he lay a-roaring
In agonies gigantic,

[174]

The lamp-oil out came pouring,
And greased the wide Atlantic.

(Would we'd been in the Navy,
And cruising there! Imagine us
All in a sea of gravy,
With billow oleaginous!)

At length old million-pounder,
Low on a bed of coral,
Gave his last dying flounder,
Whereto I pen this moral.

### MORAL

O, let this tale dramatic,
Anent the whale Norwegian
And pressure hydrostatic,
Warn you, my young collegian,

That down-compelling forces
Increase as you get deeper;
The lower down your course is,
The upward path's the steeper.

HENRY A. BEERS

## LAST LOVE

My first sweetheart was golden-haired,
Blue-eyed and seventeen;
But Ma said we were badly paired
And Ma had Beatrice so scared
That Bee was soon 'Has Been'!

My next—a little Levantine—
(Dangerous, dusky, chic,
Black-eyed, with profile aquiline)
Ran up big bills, drank gobs of wine,
And left me, for a sheik!

My third, most amorous of dames,
Dad nick-named 'Josephine',
Then—foxing me, and older flames—
Took her up West for 'fun and games'—
(They have not since been seen!)

My fourth? No! Such was my despair
I couldn't face a she:
And then, one day, the winsome air,
The bright brown eyes and tousled hair
Of Jill enchanted me.

And she adored me too, with mind
And heart, and always will.
She knows I'm master (firm but kind—
Caressed, she waggles her behind!)
My Bitch! My Puppy—Jill!

ALEXANDER SILVERLOCK

## MY DUMB FRIENDS

My home is a haven for one who enjoys
The clamour of children and ear-splitting noise
From a number of dogs who are always about,
And who want to come in and, once in, to go out.
Whenever I settle to read by the fire,

Some dog will develop an urge to retire,
And I'm constantly opening and shutting the door
For a dog to depart or, as mentioned before,
For a dog to arrive who, politely admitted,
Will make a bee-line for the chair I've just quitted.
Our friends may be dumb, but my house is a riot,
Where I cannot sit still and can never be quiet.

RALPH WOTHERSPOON

## A DUTCHMAN'S DOG STORY

Dere vhas a leedle vomans once
    Who keept a leedle shtore,
Und had a leedle puppy dog
    Dot shtoodt pefore der door.
Und evfery dime der peoples coom
    He opened vide him's jaw.
        Schnip! Schnap! shoost so,
            Und bite dem.

Vun day anoder puppy dog
    Cooms runnin' down der shtreet,
Oudt of Herr Schneider's sausage-shop,
    Vhere he had shtoled some meat;
Und after him der Schneider man—
    Der vhind vhas not more fleet.
        Whir-r-r! Whist! shoost so,
            Like vinkin!

Der leedle voman's puppy dog
    Vhas lookin' at der fun,
He barkit at der Schneider man,
    Und right pefore him run;

[177]

Den fell him down, dot Schneider man,
  Like shooted mit a gun.
    Bang! Crash! shoost so,
      Und voorser.

Der puppy dog dot shtoled der meat,
  Roon'd on und got avhay;
Der leedle voman's puppy dog
  Der Schneider man did slay,
Und make him indo sausages—
  Dot's vot der peoples say.
    Chip! Chop! shoost so,
      Und sell him.

### DER MORAL

Der moral is, don't interfere
  Vhen droubles is aroundt;
Der man dot's in der fightin' crowd
  Vhill get hurt I'll be pound.
Mind your own peesness, dot is pest,
  In life she vhill be found.
    Yaw! Yaw! shoost so,
      I pet you.

J. T. BROWN

## I HAD A DUCK-BILLED PLATYPUS

I had a duck-billed platypus when I was up at Trinity,
With whom I soon discovered a remarkable affinity.
He used to live in lodgings with myself and Arthur Purvis,
And we all went up together for the Diplomatic Service.
I had a certain confidence, I own, in his ability;
He mastered all the subjects with remarkable facility;

And Purvis, though more dubious, agreed that he was clever,
But no one else imagined he had any chance whatever.

I failed to pass the interview, The Board with wry grimaces
Objected to my boots and took exception to my braces;
And Purvis too was failed by an intolerant examiner,
Who said he had his doubts as to his sock-suspenders'
    stamina.
Our summary rejection, though we took it with urbanity,
Was naturally wounding in some measure to our vanity.
The bitterness of failure was considerably mollified,
However, by the ease with which our platypus had qualified.

The wisdom of the choice, it soon appeared, was undeniable,
There never was a diplomat more thoroughly reliable.
The creature never acted with undue precipitation O,
But gave to every question his mature consideration O.
He never made rash statements that his enemies might hold
    him to;
He never stated anything, for no one ever told him to;
And soon he was appointed, so correct was his behaviour,
Our Minister (without portfolio) in Trans Moravia.

My friend was loved and honoured from the Andes to Esthonia;
He soon achieved a pact between Peru and Patagonia;
He never vexed the Russians nor offended the Rumanians;
He pacified the Letts and he appeased the Lithuanians.
No Minister has ever worked more cautiously or slowly O;
In fact they had decided to award him a portfolio,
When, on the anniversary of Greek Emancipation,
Alas! He laid an egg in the Bulgarian Legation.

This unexpected action caused unheard-of inconvenience,
A breach at once occurred between the Turks and the
    Armenians;
The Greeks poured ultimata, quite unhinged by the mishap,
    at him;
The Poles began to threaten and the Finns began to flap at him;
The Swedes withdrew entirely from the Anglo-Saxon dailies
The right of photographing the Aurora Borealis;
And, all attempts to come to a *rapprochement* proving barren,
The Japanese in self-defence annexed the Isle of Arran.

My platypus, once thought to be more cautious and more
    tentative
Than any other living diplomatic representative,

Was now a sort of warning to all diplomatic students—
The perfect incarnation of the perils of imprudence.
Beset and persecuted by the forces of reaction O,
He reaped the consequences of his ill-considered action O;
And, branded in the Honours List as Platypus, Dame Vera,
Retired, a lonely figure, to lay eggs at Bordighera.

PATRICK BARRINGTON

*Of this poem the Director of Research, Librarian and Keeper of
the Papers, Foreign Office, said, 'While not unknown here, it has
not been found possible to identify the author'. But he has now been
identified as Patrick Barrington and the poem as No. XV of 'Songs
of a Sub-man' ('Punch', August 23rd 1933); it is here reproduced by
permission of the Proprietors of 'Punch'.*

## A SONNET ON A MONKEY

O lovely O most charming pug
Thy graceful air and heavenly mug
The beauties of his mind do shine
And every bit is shaped so fine
Your very tail is most divine
Your teeth is whiter than the snow
You are a great buck and a bow
Your eyes are of so fine a shape
More like a christians than an ape
His cheeks is like the roses blume
Your hair is like the ravens plume
His noses cast is of the roman
He is a very pretty weoman
I could not get a rhyme for roman
And was oblidged to call it weoman.

MARJORY FLEMING

'Bow' is a mis-spelling of 'beau'

[181]

*In* The Oxford Companion to English Literature *Marjory Fleming's name is given as 'Margaret Fleming' or 'Pet Marjorie'. She lived only from* 1803 *to* 1811 *and was known as a young prodigy, and the little friend of Sir Walter Scott. This little girl who died in her eighth year wrote other verses, including a poem on Mary Queen of Scots, and 'a quaint diary'. She read* The Newgate Calendar, *and said of it, 'a book that contains all the Murders: all the Murders did I say, nay all Thefts and Forgeries that ever were committed . . . is very instructive Amusing, and shews us the nesesity of doing good and not evil.'*

Some lines from

## 'TO A FISH OF THE BROOKE'

Enjoy thy stream, O harmless fish;
And when an angler for his dish,
  Through gluttony's vile sin,
Attempts, a wretch, to pull thee *out*,
God give thee strength, O gentle trout,
  To pull the raskall *in*!

JOHN WOLCOT (PETER PINDAR): 1738–1839

## BOSS SHOT

A bird, a man, a loaded gun.
No bird, dead man, Thy will be done.

ANON

## THE FROG

What a wonderful bird the frog are—
When he stand he sit almost;
When he hop, he fly almost.

[182]

He ain't got no sense hardly;
He ain't got no tail hardly either.
When he sit, he sit on what he ain't got
  almost.

ANON (FRENCH CANADIAN)

## Some lines from the poem
# 'TO MR. JOHN MOORE, AUTHOR OF THE CELEBRATED WORM-POWDER'

How much, egregious Moore, are we
  Deceived by shows and forms!
Whate'er we think, whate'er we see,
  All humankind are worms.

The learn'd themselves we book-worms name,
  The blockhead is a slow-worm;
The nymph whose tail is all on flame,
  Is aptly term'd a glow-worm:

The flatterer an earwig grows;
  Thus worms suit all conditions;
Misers are muck-worms, silk-worms beaux,
  And death-watches, physicians.

O learned friend of Abchurch Lane
  Who sett'st our entrails free!
Vain is thy art, thy powder vain,
  Since worms shall eat e'en thee.

ALEXANDER POPE

## THE GOAT

The Billy goat's a handsome gent
But has a most far-reaching scent.
The Nanny goat is quite a belle.
Let's hope she has no sense of smell.

ROLAND YOUNG

*Roland Young is the famous star of stage and screen.*

## ON A PARSON BIT BY HIS HORSE

The steed bit his master;
How came this to pass?
He heard the good pastor
Cry, 'All flesh is grass!'

OLD JINGLE

## SOMETHING TO CROW ABOUT

I sometimes think I'd rather crow
And be a rooster than to roost
And be a crow. But I dunno.

A rooster he can roost also,
Which don't seem fair when crows can't crow.
Which may help some. Still I dunno.

Crows should be glad of one thing though;
Nobody thinks of eating crow,
While roosters they are good enough
For anyone unless they're tough.

There're lots of tough old roosters though,
And anyway a crow can't crow,
So mebby roosters stand more show.
It looks that way. But I dunno.

ANON

## OCTOPUS
### *In imitation of Swinburne*

Strange beauty, eight-limbed and eight-handed,
  Whence camest to dazzle our eyes?
With thy bosom bespangled and banded
  With the hues of the seas and the skies;
Is thy home European or Asian,
  O mystical monster marine?
Part molluscous and partly crustacean,
  Betwixt and between.

Wast thou born to the sound of sea-trumpets?
  Hast thou eaten and drunk to excess
Of the sponges—thy muffins and crumpets,
  Of the seaweed—thy mustard and cress?
Wast thou nurtured in caverns of coral,
  Remote from reproof or restraint?
Art thou innocent, art thou immoral,
  Sinburnian or Saint?

Lithe limbs, curling free, as a creeper
  That creeps in a desolate place,
To enrol and envelop the sleeper
  In a silent and stealthy embrace,

[185]

Cruel beak craning forward to bite us,
    Our juices to drain and to drink,
Or to whelm us in waves of Cocytus,
    Indelible ink!

O breast, that 'twere rapture to writhe on!
    O arms 'twere delicious to feel
Clinging close with the crush of the Python,
    When she maketh her murderous meal!
In thy eight-fold embraces enfolden,
    Let our empty existence escape;
Give us death that is glorious and golden,
    Crushed all out of shape!

Ah! thy red lips, lascivious and luscious,
    With death in their amorous kiss!
Cling round us, and clasp us, and crush us,
    With bitings of agonized bliss;
We are sick with the poison of pleasure,
    Dispense us the potion of pain;
Ope thy mouth to its uttermost measure
    And bite us again!

                                    A. C. HILTON: 1851–77

# The Frolicsome Kick of the Limerick

\* \* \* \* \* \* \* \* \* \* \* \* \* \* \* \* \* \* \* \* \* \*

*Since the days of Edward Lear, who popularized the Limerick as
a form, his motley followers have amazingly improved upon it.
Although it is the fashion nowadays to crack up Lear, the plain fact
is that the best of his Limericks are amateurish compared with modern
efforts. The orthodox Lear's 'Vain Repetition' in the final line of
the last word in his first line was his earthbound limitation. He even
failed, often enough, to spring a double meaning or to put some other
kick into his last line, although he did so in:*

> There was an Old Man with a beard
> Who said, 'It is just as I feared!—
>     Four Larks and a Wren,
>     Two Owls and a Hen,
> Have all built their nests in my beard!'

*And:*

> There was a Young Lady of Ryde,
> Whose shoe-strings were seldom untied;
>     She purchased some clogs
>     And some small spotty dogs
> And frequently *walked* about *Ryde.*

*These (with my italics)—acknowledged as two of Lear's best—can't
hold a candle to the anonymous modern:*

There was an old fellow of Lympne
Who married three wives at one time;
   When asked: 'Why the third?'
   He replied, 'One's absurd;
And bigamy, Sir, is a crime.'

*Or—for those purists who asseverate that Lympne should be pro-nounced 'Limb':*

There was an old fellow of Lympne,
Who said, 'How I wish I was slim!'
   So he lived for three weeks
   On a nut and two leeks
And that was the last heard of him.

*Still, the lightsome lilt of the modern, or revised version, relies quite a lot on the original Learish scansion and line indentation—and, if one is asked why, one might answer in the words of another unknown poet:*

Well, it's partly the shape of the thing
That gives the old limerick swing:
These accordion pleats
Full of airy conceits
Take it up like a kite on the wing.

*In the good old days of Prohibition hospitable American hosts used to mix a drink of LIME-RICKY plus Bath-tub Gin. This looks reminiscent, but was pronounced Lime (as in lime)—not Limb (as in limerick). The mixture certainly gave one a lightsome lilt before laying one out in 'accordion pleats'. And it would have been better named Limb-ricky!*

*Here there are less than ·0005 per cent of known extant limericks, and readers are requested not to encourage propagation of the species. As it is, scores are being spawned daily. They are hardy, and of those extant few become extinct. Some of the earliest anonymous efforts—like the young lady of Niger who smiled as she rode on a tiger—are still known to about one-third of the human race. Apropos of which rapid piece of mental arithmetic there comes to mind the story of the woman who was reading snippets from the evening paper to her husband:*

'Gosh, George! It says here that every third child born into the world is Chinese!'

'Thank Gawd,' says George, 'we only got two!'

## MANNERS

There was a young lady of Tottenham,
Who'd no manners, or else she'd forgotten 'em;

At tea at the vicar's
She tore off her knickers
Because, she explained, she felt 'ot in 'em.

ANON

## ORTALITYM

A silly young fellow named Hyde
In a funeral procession was spied;
    When asked, 'Who is dead?'
    He giggled and said,
'I don't know; I just came for the ride.'

ANON

## MUSIC

There was an old person of Tring
Who, when somebody asked her to sing,
    Replied, 'Ain't it odd?
    I can never tell *God
Save the Weasel* from *Pop Goes the King!*'

ANON

## THE LATE LAMENTED

A novice was driving a car,
When, down Porlock, his son said, 'Papa,
    If you drive at this rate
    We are bound to be *late*—
Drive faster!'—He did, and they are!

ANON

## DOUBLE INTERMENT

There was a young fellow from Clyde
Who fell down a sewer and died.
 The next day his brother
 Fell into another
So now they're interred side by side.

ANON

## MAL DE MER?

There was a fair maid of Ostend
Who thought she'd hold out to the end
 But half the way over
 'Twixt Calais and Dover
She did what she didn't intend.

ANON

## THE LOST WEEKEND

There was a young lady from Joppa
Who came a Society cropper
 She went to Ostend
 With a gentleman friend
And the rest of the story's improper.

ANON

## DO NOT SPIT

There was an old man of Darjeeling
Who travelled from London to Ealing
 It said on the door,
 'Please don't spit on the floor,'
So he carefully spat on the ceiling.  ANON

# Gay Yet Wistful

★ ★ ★ ★ ★ ★ ★ ★ ★ ★ ★ ★ ★ ★ ★ ★ ★ ★ ★ ★ ★

*First let us linger over Leland's little-known classic in Pidgin-English,* The Princess in Tartary.

*The Princess, as daughter (kai) of the Chinese Emperor (Pili), has for political reasons been given in marriage to the King of the Cold (Colo) Land, Tartary, and she is homesick and cries (makee cly-cly) for the protecting warmth of her mother's arms:*

## THE PRINCESS IN TARTARY

Belongey China Empelor,
   My make one piecee sing:
He catchee one cow-chilo,
   She waifo Tartar King,
Hab lib in colo lan',
   Hab stop where ice belong,
What-tim much solly in-i-sy
   She makee t'his sing-song:
    "He wind he wailo 'way.
    He wind he wailo long,
An' bleeze blow ovely almon'-tlee,
    An' cally a birdo song.

---

cow-chilo: daughter.    colo lan': cold country, i.e. Tartary.    solly: in grief.
in-i-sy: inside; not in common use, but given in this form in Chinese vocabulary. *In-sy* is, however, sometimes heard.
                wailo: goes.    cally: carry.

"Too muchee li to China-side
  T'hat place he tlee glow high,
My fàta blongey palacee,
  All golo in-i-sy
My wantchee look-see màta,
  He màta wantchee kai,
My tinkey Mongol fashiono
  No plopa fashion my.
    Ai! wind he wailo 'way,
    Ai! wind he wailo long,
An' bleeze blow ovely almon'-tlee,
  An' cally a birdo song!"


He birdo wailo Pay-chin
  Chop-chop he makee fly;
T'hat màta hear he sing-song,
  How muchee dàta cly,
How Tartar-side he colo,
  How muchee nicee warm,
One dàta-chilo catchee
  In-i-sy he màta arm.
    Ai! wind he wailo 'way,
    Ai! wind he wailo long,
An' bleeze blow ovely almon'-tlee,
  An' cally a birdo song.


"He go top-sidee cow,
  T'hat fashion Tartar-side,
T'hat no be plopa fashion
  For Pili-kai to lide.

li: a Chinese mile (pronounced 'lee').    fàta: father.    golo inisy; gold
inside.    màta; mother.    kai: daughter.    plopa; proper.
Pay-chin; Peking.    chop-chop; quickly.    in-i-sy: inside, within, in.
pili-kai; Emperor's daughter.

Supposee he lib homo,
　So-fashion he look-see,
He *li*de fo' piecee horsey
　In coachey galantee.
　　Ai! wind he wailo 'way,
　　Ai! wind he wailo long,
An' b*l*eeze blow ove*l*y almon'-t*l*ee,
　　An' ca*ll*y he birdo song."

He mata talkee Pili:
　He Pili open han',
He talkee, "No good fashion
　Hab got in Tartar lan'.
Must make one China town,
　Must makee for he kai;
Must makee Tartar-sidee,
　An' he no makee c*l*y."
　　Ai! wind he wailo 'way
　　Ai! wind he wailo long,
An' b*l*eeze blow ove*l*y almon'-t*l*ee,
　　An' ca*ll*y he birdo song.

He sendee muchee coolie,
　He sendee smartee man,
He makee China city
　In-i-sy t'hat Tartar lan'.
He kai catch p*l*opa palace
　An' coachey galantee,
No more hab makee c*l*y-c*l*y.
　My sing-song finishee.

lide: ride

[194]

Ai! wind he wailo 'way,
Ai! wind he wailo long,
An' *b*leeze blow ove*ly* almon'-t*lee*,
An' ca*lly* he birdo song.

CHARLES G. LELAND

### RELEASE

The youthful shapes that please my eyes
  No longer plague my heart.
Mild Age disarms and sanctifies
The youthful shapes that please my eyes.
Like strains of heavenly music rise
  And harmlessly depart
The youthful shapes that please—my eyes
No longer plague my heart.

OSWALD COULDREY

*Quoted from 'Triolets and Epigrams' by kind permission of the Author and the Abbey Press, Abingdon.*

## FROM THE TOMBSTONE OF A CAT
## MEAFORD HALL, NEAR STONE,
## STAFFORDSHIRE

'Tis false that all of Pussy's Race
Regard not person, but the Place,
For here lies one, who, could She tell
Her stories by some magic spell
Would from the quitted barn and grove,
Her sporting haunts, to show her love
At sound of footsteps absent long
Of those she soothed with purring song,

[195]

Leap to their arms in fond embrace,
For love of them, and not for Place.

EARL ST. VINCENT

## THE INTRO

'Er name's Doreen. . . Well, spare me bloomin' days!
   You could 'a' knocked me down wiv 'arf a brick!
Yes, me, that kids meself I know their ways,
   An' 'as a name for smoogin' in our click!
I jist lines up an' tips the saucy wink.
But strike! The way she piled on dawg! Yeh'd think
   A bloke wus givin' back-chat to the Queen. . . .
      'Er name's Doreen.


I seen 'er in the markit first uv all,
Inspectin' brums at Steeny Isaacs' stall.
   I backs me barrer in—the same ole way—
   An' sez, 'Wot O! It's been a bonzer day.
'Ow is it fer a walk?'. . . Oh, 'oly wars!
The sort o' *look* she gimme! Jest becors
   I tried to chat 'er, like yeh'd make a start
      Wiv *any* tart.


An' I kin take me oaf I wus perlite,
An' never said no word that wasn't right,
   An' never tried to maul 'er, or to do
   A thing yeh might call crook. Ter tell yeh true,
I didn't seem to 'ave the nerve—wiv 'er.
I felt as if I couldn't go that fur,
   An' start to sling off chiack like I used . . .
      *Not intrajuiced!*

[196]

Nex' time I sighted 'er in Little Bourke,
Where she wus in a job. I found 'er lurk
   Wus pastin' labels in a pickle joint,
    A game that—any'ow, that ain't the point.
Once more I tried to chat 'er in the street,
But, bli'me! Did she turn me down a treat!
   The way she tossed 'er 'ead an' swished her skirt!
    Oh, it was dirt!

A squarer tom I swear, I never seen,
In all me natchril, than this 'ere Doreen.
   It wer'n't no guyver neither: fer I knoo
    That any other bloke 'ad Buckley's 'oo
Tried fer to pick 'er up. Yes, she wus square.
She jist sailed by an' lef' me standin' there
   Like any mug. Thinks I, 'I'm out o' luck,'
    An' done a duck.

Well, I dunno. It's that way wiv a bloke.
If she'd a' breasted up to me an' spoke,
   I'd thort 'er jist a common bit o' fluff,
    An' then fergot about 'er, like enough.
It's jist like this. The tarts that's 'ard ter get
Makes you all 'ot to chase 'em, and to let
   The cove called Cupid git an 'ammer-lock;
    An' lose yer block.

I know a bloke 'oo knows a bloke 'oo toils
In that same pickle found-cry. ('E boils
   The cabbitch storks or somethink.) Anyway,
    I gives me pal the orfis fer to say
'E 'as a sister in the trade 'oo's been
Out uv a job, an' wants to meet Doreen;

Then we kin get an intro, if we've luck.
　'E sez, 'Ribuck.'


O' course we worked the oricle; you bet!
But, 'struth, I ain't recovered frum it yet!
　'Twas on a Saturdee night, in Colluns Street,
　An'—quite be accident, o' course—we meet.
Me pal 'e trots 'er up an' does the toff—
'E allus wus a bloke fer showin' off.
　　'This 'ere's Doreen,' 'e sez. 'This 'ere's the Kid.'
　　I dips me lid.


'This 'ere's Doreen,' 'e sez. I sez 'Good day.'
An' bli'me, I 'ad nothin' more ter say!
　I couldn't speak a word, or meet 'er eye.
　Clean done me block! I never bin so shy,
Not since I wus a tiny little cub,
An' run the rabbit to the corner pub—
　　Wot time the Summer days wus dry an' 'ot—
　　Fer my ole pot.


Me! that 'as barracked tarts, an' torked an' larft,
An' chucked orf at 'em like a phonergraft!
　Gawstruth! I seemed to lose me pow'r o' speech.
　But 'er! Oh, strike me pink! She is a peach!
The sweetest in the barrer! Spare me days,
I carn't describe that cliner's winnin' ways.
　　The way she torks! 'Er lips! 'Er eyes! 'Er hair! . . .
　　Oh, gimme air!


I dunno 'ow I done it in the end.
I rekerlect I arst to be 'er friend;

An' tried to play at 'andies in the park,
A thing she wouldn't sight. Aw, it's a nark!
I gotter swear when I think wot a mug
I must 'a' seemed to 'er. But still I 'ug
   That promise that she give me fer the beach.
    The bonzer peach!


Now, as the poit sez, the days drag by
On ledding feet. I wish't they'd do a guy.
   I dunno 'ow I 'ad the nerve ter speak,
    An' make that meet wiv 'er fer Sund'y week!
But strike! It's funny wot a bloke'll do
When 'e's all out . . . She's gorn, when I come-to.
   I'm yappin' to me cobber uv me mash . . .
    I've done me dash!


'Er name's Doreen. . . An' me—that thort I knoo
   The ways uv tarts, an' all that smoogin' game!
An' so I ort; fer ain't I known a few?
   Yet some 'ow . . . I dunno. It ain't the same.
I carn't tell *wot* it is, but all I know,
I've dropped me bundle—an' I'm glad it's so.
   Fer when I come ter think uv wot I been . . .
    'Er name's Doreen.

C. J. DENNIS (AUSTRALIA)

*C. J. Dennis has written a delightful dictionary of the slang used in his poems, but Sydney is so close to Seven Dials—(well!—in dialect, anyway)—that few definitions are really essential.*

*Here are some of the stickiest:*

*Smoogin': to bill and coo; Brums: tawdry finery (from Brummagem—Birmingham); Chiack: vulgar banter; Lurk: regular occupation; Guyver: make-believe; Buckley's (chance): a forlorn hope; Ribuck: correct, O.K.—And might have come from 'Right, Buck!'—an easy term to translate. The rest should be easy enough too, except, perhaps, for Statcher: a statue.*

## PILOT COVE

'Young friend,' 'e sez . . . Young friend! Well spare
  me days!
    Yeh'd think I wus 'is own white-'eaded boy—
The queer ole finger, wiv 'is gentle ways.
    'Young friend,' 'e sez, 'I wish't yeh bofe great joy.'
    The langwidge that them parson blokes imploy
Fair tickles me. The way 'e bleats an' brays!
        'Young friend,' 'e sez.

'Young friend,' 'e sez . . . Yes, my Doreen an' me
  We're gettin' hitched, all straight an' on the square,
Fer when I torks about the registry—
  O 'oly wars! yeh should 'a' seen 'er stare;
  'The registry?' she sez, 'I wouldn't dare!
I know a clergyman we'll go an' see'. . .
        'Young friend,' 'e sez.

'Young friend,' 'e sez. An' then 'e chats me straight;
  An' spouts uv death, an' 'ell, an' mortal sins.
'You reckernize this step you contemplate
  Is grave?' 'e sez. An' I jist stan's an' grins;
  Fer when I chips, Doreen she kicks me shins.
'Yes, very 'oly is the married state,
        Young friend,' 'e sez.

[200]

'Young friend,' 'e sez. An' then 'e mags a lot
　　Of jooty an' the spiritchuil life,
To which I didn't tumble worth a jot.
　　'I'm sure', 'e sez, 'as you will 'ave a wife
　　'Oo'll 'ave a noble infl'ince on yer life.
'Oo is 'er gardjin?' I sez, ' 'Er ole pot'—
　　　　'Young friend!' 'e sez.


'Young friend,' 'e sez, 'Oh fix yer thorts on 'igh!
　　Orl marriages is registered up there!
An' you must cleave unto 'er till yeh die,
　　An' cherish 'er wiv love an' tender care.
　　E'en in the days when she's no longer fair
She's still yer wife,' 'e sez. 'Ribuck,' sez I.
　　　　*'Young friend!'* 'e sez.


'Young friend,' 'e sez—I sez, 'Now listen 'ere:
　　This isn't one o' them impetchus leaps.
There ain't no tart a 'undredth part so dear
　　As 'er. She 'as me 'eart an' soul fer keeps!'
　　An' then Doreen, she turns away an' weeps;
But 'e jist smiles. 'Yer deep in love, 'tis clear,
　　　　Young friend,' 'e sez.


'Young friend,' 'e sez—an' tears wus in 'is eyes—
　　'Strive 'ard. For many, many years I've lived.
An' I kin but recall wiv tears an' sighs
　　The lives of some I've seen in marridge gived,'
　　'My Gawd!' I sez. 'I'll strive as no bloke strivved!
Fer don't I know I've copped a bonzer prize?'
　　　　'Young friend,' 'e sez.

'Young friend,' 'e sez. An' in 'is gentle way
   'E pats the shoulder uv my dear Doreen,
'I've solim'ized grand weddin's in me day,
   But 'ere's the sweetest little maid I've seen.
   She's fit fer any man, to be 'is queen;
An' you're more forchinit than you kin say,
      Young friend!' 'e sez.

'Young friend,' 'e sez . . . A queer old pilot bloke
   Wiv silver 'air. The gentle way 'e dealt
Wiv 'er, the soft an' kindly way 'e spoke
   To my Doreen, 'ud make a statcher melt.
   I tell yeh, square an' all. I sort o' felt
A kiddish kind o' feelin' like I'd choke . . .
      'Young friend,' 'e sez.

'Young friend,' 'e sez, 'you two on Choosday week,
   Is to be joined in very 'oly bonds.
To break them vows I 'opes yeh'll never seek;
   Fer I could curse them 'usbands 'oo absconds!'
   'I'll love 'er till I snuff it,' I responds.
'Ah, that's the way I likes to 'ear yeh speak,
      Young friend,' 'e sez.

'Young friend,' 'e sez—an' then me 'and 'e grips—
   'I wish't yeh luck, you an' yer lady fair.
Sweet maid.' An' sof'ly wiv 'is finger-tips,
   'E takes an' strokes me cliner's shinin' 'air.
   An' when I seen 'er standin' blushin' there,
I turns an' kisses 'er, fair on the lips.
      'Young friend!' 'e sez.

C. J. DENNIS (AUSTRALIA)

## YAWCOB STRAUSS

I haf von funny leedle poy,
Vot gomes schust to mine knee;
Der queerest schap, der createst rogue,
As efer you dit see.
He runs, und schumps, und schmashes dings
In all barts of der house;
But vot off dat? he vas mine son,
Mine leedle Yawcob Strauss.

He get der measles und der mumbs,
Und eferyding dot's oudt;
He sbills mine glass of lager bier,
Poots schnuff indo mine kraut.
He fills mine pipe mit limburg cheese—
Dot vas der roughest chouse;
I'd dake dot vrom no oder poy
But leedle Yawcob Strauss.

He dakes der milk-ban for a dhrum,
And cuts mine cane in dwo,
To make der schticks to beat it mit—
Mine gracious, dot vos drue!
I dinks mine hed was schplit abart,
He kicks oup sooch a touse:
But never mind; der poys vas few
Like dot young Yawcob Strauss.

He asks me questions, sooch as dese:
Who baints mine nose so red?
Who vas it cuts dot schmoodth blace oudt
Vrom der hair ubon mine hed?

Und uhere der blaze goes vrom der lamp
Vene'er der glim I douse.
How gan I all dose dings eggsblain
To dot schmall Yawcob Strauss.

I somedimes dink I schall go vild
Mit sooch a grazy poy,
Und vish vonce more I gould haf rest,
Und beaceful dimes enshoy;
But ven he vash asleep in ped,
So guiet as a mouse,
I prays der Lord, 'Dake anyding,
But leaf dot Yawcob Strauss.'

CHARLES FOLLEN ADAMS

## A PATHETIC PSYCHE

The hyperaesthetic schizoid type
Is given to talking and writing tripe.
They go all timid and hide in holes,
And even worry about their souls.
Though not religious, they like to talk
Of metaphysics. They never walk
With striding gait and aspect free,
But read a book beneath a tree.
Obsessed with doubt, they cannot find
Comfort in heart or soul or mind.
They long for companions, yearn for a friend,
But find only bitterness at the end.
They spend whole days in bleak despair,
Grow happy when the sun shines fair,
Ecstatic at the birth of Spring:
The bright dark eye and fluttering wing

Of every bird is their delight—
They almost feel their souls take flight
To join the essential harmony
Of sky and field, and hill and sea.
But something always drags them back
To their unhappy selves. The black
And sullen mood returns once more,
More black and sullen than before.
What can be done with hearts like these?
Will death at last afford them ease?
Will they sleep then, as before birth,
Silence their friend, their blanket earth?

WINIFRED AMBLER

## THE HONEYMOON ANNIVERSARY

The skyline smoke veers—veers and dims
As unpredictable as your whims—
The planing seagull rockets by
With your identical watchful eye;
And everything—within, without—
Shakes to your voice, or the West wind's shout.
Is there no peace—no kindly thought—
In this damned holiday resort?
At night, when quiet falls serene,
You'll snore like a foundering submarine;
And I'll lie still and watch the stars
Steal past the shuddering window-bars:
Cold stars, whose rays across the years
Impartial glint, on dew—or tears.

ARNOLD SILCOCK

## LESS GAY THAN WISTFUL

True is the saying, that in common lives
There dies a poet and the man survives.

.  .  .  .  .  .

In some he dies hard, and, before he dies,
Keeps in the half-extinguished spirit-eyes
Just sight enough to know he cannot see;
And so the poet that still breathes in me
And strives his fitful essence to prolong,
Once, to the joy departing, made this song.

ANON

## THE LOOK

Strephon kissed me in the spring,
   Robin in the fall,
But Colin only looked at me
   And never kissed at all.

Strephon's kiss was lost in jest,
   Robin's lost in play,
But the kiss in Colin's eyes
   Haunts me night and day.

SARA TEASDALE

## 'LA VIE'

La vie est vaine,
Un peu d'amour,
Un peu de haine
Et puis—bonjour!

[206]

La vie est brève,
Un peu d'espoir,
Un peu de rêve,
Et puis—bonsoir!

LEON MONTENAEKEN

# The Lunatic Fringe

★ ★ ★ ★ ★ ★ ★ ★ ★ ★ ★ ★ ★ ★ ★ ★ ★ ★ ★ ★

*Trailing clouds of glory we have come—perhaps—and as serious mortals (now grown, maybe, to bilious bachelorhood) we could never enjoy the following ephemeral and fantastic effusions.*

*On the other hand, you may have come trailing crowds of story-book airy-fairies from the lunatic fringe of Cloud-Cuckoo Land. Then you will agree with the elect—the emancipated minority—that nothing is more delightful as crackpottery than the crazy genius of slightly cracked poetry—thus:*

## TO WILLIAM HAYLEY

Thy Friendship oft has made my heart to ache:
Do be my enemy, for Friendship's sake.

*This frenzied plea was pled by . . .*

WILLIAM BLAKE

## AESTIVATION

In candent ire the solar splendor flames;
The foles, languescent, pend from arid rames;
His humid front the cive, anheling, wipes,
And dreams of erring on ventiferous ripes.

How dulce to vive occult to mortal eyes,
Dorm on the herb with none to supervise,

[208]

Carp the suave berries from the crescent vine,
And bibe the flow from longicaudate kine!

To me, alas! no verdurous visions come,
Save yon exiguous pool's confervascum,—
No concave vast repeats the tender hue
That laves my milk-jug with celestial blue!

Me wretched! Let me curr to quercine shades!
Effund your albid hausts, lactiferous maids!
O, might I vole to some umbrageous clump,—
Depart,—be off,—excede,—evade,—erump!

OLIVER WENDELL HOLMES

## GOINGS ON OF AN ALTER EGO

Oh, when I was above myself
    I was a curious pair;
My lower feet still walked the street,
    My uppers trod on air.
Said folk 'You must come down a peg,
    We know not where you stand';
So reaching up I pulled my leg
    And took myself in hand.

Oh, when I was beside myself
    I doubled through the town
And sober men who saw me then
    Crept home and laid them down.
But all the neighbours raised a groan
    To view my brace of chins;
Said folk 'We love you best alone:
    You're just a mess as twins.'

[209]

And now I march in twos no more;
   I keep myself inside,
And Jekyll rests as heretofore
   Imprisoned in his Hyde.
Yet when they read this little rhyme
   I know what folk will say:
They will most surely say that I'm
   Below myself to-day.

M. H. LONGSON

From *Punch*, 9th February 1949

## THE PARTERRE

I don't know any greatest treat
As sit him in a gay parterre,
And sniff one up the perfume sweet
Of every roses buttoning there.

It only want my charming miss
Who make to blush the self red rose;
Oh! I have envy of to kiss
The end's tip of her splendid nose.

Oh! I have envy of to be
What grass 'neath her pantoffle push,
And too much happy seemeth me
The margaret which her vestige crush.

But I will meet her nose at nose,
And take occasion for her hairs,
And indicate her all my woes,
That she in fine agree my prayers.

[210]

> I don't know any greatest treat
> As sit him in a gay parterre,
> With Madame who is too more sweet
> Than every roses buttoning there.
>
> E. H. PALMER: 1840–82

## THE BARBER'S NUPTIALS

In Liquorpond Street, as is well known to many,
An artist resided, who shaved for a penny,
Cut hair for three halfpence, for threepence he bled,
And would draw for a groat every tooth in your head.

What annoy'd other folks never spoil'd his repose,
'Twas the same thing to him whether stocks fell or
    rose:
For blast and for mildew he cared not a pin,
His crops never fail'd, for they grew on the chin.

Unvex'd by the cares that ambition and state has,
Contented he dined on his daily potatoes;
And the pence that he earn'd by excision of bristle,
Were nightly devoted to wetting his whistle. . . .

But Cupid, who trims men of every station,
And 'twixt barbers and beaux makes no discrimination,
Would not let this superlative shaver alone,
Till he tried if his heart was as hard as his hone.

The fair one, whose charms did the barber enthral,
At the end of Fleet Market, of fish kept a stall,
As red as her cheek, was no lobster e'er seen;
Not an eel that she sold was so soft as her skin.

By love strange effects have been wrought, we are told,
In all countries and climates, hot, temp'rate, or cold;
Thus the heart of our barber love scorch'd like a coal,
Though 'tis very well known he lived under the *pole*.

First, he courted his charmer in sorrowful fashion,
And lied like a lawyer, to move her compassion:
He should perish, he swore, did his suit not succeed,
And a barber to slay was a barbarous deed. . . .

Indignant, she answer'd, 'No chin-scraping sot
Shall be fasten'd to me by the conjugal knot;
No! to Tyburn repair, if a noose you must tie,
Other fish I have got, Mr. Tonsor, to fry:

'Holborn-bridge and Blackfriars' my triumphs can tell,
From Billingsgate beauties I've long borne the bell:
Nay, tripe-men and fishmongers vie for my favour;
Then d'ye think I'd take up with a two-penny shaver?

'Let dory, or turbot, the sov'reign of fish,
Cheek by jowl with red herring be served in one dish,
Let sturgeon and sprats in one pickle unite,
When I angle for husbands, and barbers shall bite.'

But the barber persisted (ah! could I relate 'em)
To ply her with compliments soft as pomatum:
And took every occasion to flatter and praise her,
Till she fancied his wit was as keen as his razor. . . .

With fair speeches cajoled, as you tickle a trout,
'Gainst the barber the fish-wife no more could hold out:

He applied the right bait, and with flatt'ry he caught her:
With flatt'ry a female's a fish out of water.

The state of her heart when the barber once guess'd,
Love's siege with redoubled exertion he press'd,
And as briskly bestirr'd him, the charmer embracing,
As the wash-ball that dances and froths in the basin.

The flame to allay their bosoms did so burn,
They set out for the church of St. Andrew in Holborn,
Where tonsors and trulls, country Dicks and their
cousins,
In the halter of wedlock are tied up by dozens. . . .

Mussel-mongers, and oyster-men, crimps and coal-
heavers,
And butchers, with marrow-bones smiting their cleavers:
Shrimp-scalders and mole-catchers, tailors and tilers,
Boys, butchers, brawls, bailiffs, and black-pudding
boilers—

From their voices united such melody flow'd
As the Abbey ne'er witness'd, nor Tott'nham-Court-
road;
While St. Andrews's bells did so loud and so clear ring,
You'd given ten pound to've been out of their hearing.

For his fee, when the parson this couple had join'd,
As no cash was forthcoming, he took it in kind:
So the bridegroom dismantled his reverence's chin,
And the bride entertained him with pilchards and gin.

ANON: EIGHTEENTH CENTURY

## THE HEIGHT OF THE RIDICULOUS

I wrote some lines, once on a time,
　In wondrous merry mood,
And thought, as usual, men would say
　They were exceeding good.

They were so queer, so very queer,
　I laugh'd as I would die;
Albeit, in the general way,
　A sober man am I.

I call'd my servant, and he came;
　How kind it was of him,
To mind a slender man like me,
　He of the mighty limb!

'These to the printer,' I exclaim'd,
　And, in my humorous way,
I added (as a trifling jest),
　'There'll be the devil to pay'.

He took the paper, and I watch'd,
　And saw him peep within;
At the first line he read, his face
　Was all upon the grin.

He read the next; the grin grew broad,
　And shot from ear to ear;
He read the third; a chuckling noise
　I now began to hear.

[214]

The fourth; he broke into a roar;
   The fifth; his waistband split;
The sixth; he burst five buttons off,
   And tumbled in a fit.

Ten days and nights, with sleepless eye,
   I watch'd that wretched man,
And since, I never dare to write
   As funny as I can.

OLIVER WENDELL HOLMES

# SONNET FOUND IN A DESERTED MAD-HOUSE

Oh that my soul a marrow-bone might seize!
For the old egg of my desire is broken,
Spilled is the pearly white and spilled the yolk, and
As the mild melancholy contents grease
My path the shorn lamb baas like bumblebees.
Time's trashy purse is as a taken token
Or like a thrilling recitation, spoken
By mournful mouths filled full of mirth and cheese.

And yet, why should I clasp the earthful urn?
Or find the frittered fig that felt the fast?
Or choose to chase the cheese around the churn?
Or swallow any pill from out the past?
Ah, no Love, not while your hot kisses burn
Like a potato riding on the blast.

ANON: NINETEENTH CENTURY

Lines from
## SAYING NOT MEANING

If you will say impossibles are true,
    You may affirm just anything you please—
That swans are quadrupeds, and lions blue,
    And elephants inhabit Stilton cheese!

                WILLIAM BASIL WAKE

And; Some Lines from
## THE IMAGINATIVE CRISIS
by an Anonymous Poet

The spell is wrought: imagination swells
My sleeping-room to hills, and woods, and dells!
I walk abroad, for naught my footsteps hinder,
And fling my arms. Oh! mi! I've broke the
       *winder*.

## THE AMERICAN INDIAN

There once were some people called Sioux
Who spent all their time making shioux
Which they coloured in various hioux;
Don't think that they made them to ioux
Oh! no, they just sold them for bioux.

           ANON: NINETEENTH CENTURY

## THE SORROWS OF WERTHER

Werther had a love for Charlotte
Such as words could never utter;
Would you know how first he met her?
She was cutting bread and butter.

Charlotte was a married lady,
And a moral man was Werther,
And for all the wealth of Indies,
Would do nothing for to hurt her.

So he sigh'd and pined and ogled,
And his passion boil'd and bubbled,
Till he blew his silly brains out,
And no more was by it troubled.

Charlotte, having seen his body
Borne before her on a shutter,
Like a well-conducted person,
Went on cutting bread and butter.

WILLIAM MAKEPEACE THACKERAY

## THE PERFECT REACTIONARY

As I was sitting in my chair
I *knew* the bottom wasn't there,
Nor legs nor back, but *I just sat*,
Ignoring little things like that.

HUGHES MEARNS

From *Alice's Adventures in Wonderland*
## EVIDENCE READ BY THE WHITE RABBIT AT THE TRIAL OF THE KNAVE OF HEARTS

They told me you had been to her,
And mentioned me to him:
She gave me a good character,
But said I could not swim.

He sent them word I had not gone
    (We know it to be true):
If I should push the matter on,
    What would become of you?

I gave her one, they gave him two,
    You gave us three or more;
They all returned from him to you,
    Though they were mine before.

If I or she should chance to be
    Involved in this affair,
He trusts to you to set them free,
    Exactly as we were.

My notion was that you had been
    (Before she had this fit)
An obstacle that came between
    Him, and ourselves, and it.

Don't let him know she liked them best,
    For this must ever be
A secret, kept from all the rest,
    Between yourself and me.

LEWIS CARROLL

## A PLAY ON WORDS

Assert ten barren love day made
    Dan woo'd her hart buy nigh tan day;
Butt wen knee begged she'd marry hymn,
    The crewel bell may dancer neigh.
Lo atter fee tin vein he side

Ant holder office offal pane—
A lasses mown touched knot terse sole—
His grown was sever awl Lynn vane.

'Owe, beam my bride, my deer, rye prey,
  And here mice size beef ore rye dye;
Oak caste mean knot tin scorn neigh way—
  Yew are the apple love me nigh!'
She herd Dan new we truly spoke.
  Key was of noble berth, and bread
Tool lofty mean and hie renown,
  The air too great testates, 't was head.

'Ewe wood due bettor, sir,' she bald,
  'Took court sum mother girl, lie wean—
Ewer knot mice stile, lisle never share
  The thrown domestic azure quean!'
' 'Tis dun, no fare butt Scilly won—
  Aisle waist know father size on the!'
Oft tooth the nay bring porte tea flue
  And through himself into the see.

EUGENE FIELD

## LONGING

I wish I was a little grub
With whiskers round my tummy
I'd climb into a honey-pot
And make my tummy gummy.

ANON

*Alleged to have been a signal sent by a naval officer during the war in one of those long intervals of boredom.*

[219]

# Whimsies

✶ ✶ ✶ ✶ ✶ ✶ ✶ ✶ ✶ ✶ ✶ ✶ ✶ ✶ ✶ ✶ ✶ ✶ ✶ ✶ ✶ ✶ ✶ ✶ ✶

*Introductory Whimsy from a Chair on the Boulevard.*

*In Paris, where I long to be, all the best things in life are free; so,
take a chair on the boulevard and watch les Parisiennes promenade:
the dainty dark-eyed midinettes, the bold cocottes and the chic co-
quettes, while Latins dark and Latins fair without remark regard
your stare, and mind not in the very least les yeux and their bon
marché feast: The sights! the songs! that take the air—'Il est Cocu,
le Chef de Gare!'—as lights go up gay voices sing, and glass and*

*cup and laughter ring. . . . Sept heures et demie. Alors—dîner!
'Garçon!—l'addition, s'il vous plaît!'—you'll dine to-night at eight
o'clock; the whole show's cost you just un bock! . . . Then, revien-
drai, back to see those good things which in France are free—le
Bois, les girls, la chance to spoon with mademoiselle, au clair de la
lune.—O chérie! O my Gay Paree! What's Home Sweet Home to
you?—or me!*

ARD SLOK

## TO A LADY WHO WANTED A PENNY
## FOR TWO HA'PENNIES

Look lidy, foller Olive Snell,
To 'oom yore accident befell.
It 'appened, as it does to many,
That *Olive* went to spend a penny.

She searched 'er bag, and 'ad jist one—
An' that wus bent—so wot she done?
She went an' found a spinney shidy . . .
*An'* saved 'erself the penny, lidy!

ARD SLOK

## ADIPOSE AUNTIE'S POSE

Auntie always was morose
And her views on life were bitter,
For she was so adipose
No ordinary seat would fit 'er:
Now I should think that *you'd* feel glum
If you'd been born with Auntie's sitter!

ANON

[221]

## WHAT IS A BASKET?

'Oh, Daddy dear, what is a basket?'
Said a youthful and mischievous elf;
'All baskets, me boy, are children of joy,
In fact you're a basket yourself!'

ANON

## I BENDED UNTO ME

I bended unto me a bough of May,
That I might see and smell:
It bore it in a sort of way,
It bore it very well.
But when I let it backward sway,
Then it were hard to tell
With what a toss, with what a swing,
The dainty thing
Resumed its proper level,
And sent me to the devil.
I know it did—you doubt it?
I turned, and saw them whispering about it.

T. E. BROWN

## THE BISHOP'S LAST DIRECTIONS

Tell my Priests, when I am gone,
O'er me to shed no tears,
For I shall be no deader then
Than they have been for years.

ANON

[222]

## THE PESSIMIST

Nothing to do but work!
Nothing! alas, alack!
Nowhere to go but out!
Nowhere to come but back!

TRADITIONAL

## THE THEATRE

'Tis sweet to view, from half-past five to six,
Our long wax-candles, with short cotton wicks,
Touch'd by the lamplighter's Promethean art,
Start into light, and make the lighter start;
To see red Phoebus through the gallery-pane
Tinge with his beam the beams of Drury Lane;
While gradual parties fill our widen'd pit,
And gape, and gaze, and wonder, ere they sit.

At first while vacant seats give choice and ease,
Distant or near, they settle where they please;
But when the multitude contracts the span,
And seats are rare, they settle where they can.
Now the full benches to late-comers doom
No room for standing, miscall'd *standing room*.

Hark! the check-taker moody silence breaks,
And bawling 'Pit full!' gives the check he takes;
Yet onward still the gathering numbers cram,
Contending crowders shout the frequent damn,
And all is bustle, squeeze, row, jabbering, and jam.

See to their desks Apollo's sons repair—
Swift rides the rosin o'er the horse's hair!
In unison their various tones to tune,
Murmurs the hautboy, growls the hoarse bassoon;
In soft vibration sighs the whispering lute,
Tang goes the harpsichord, too-too the flute,
Brays the loud trumpet, squeaks the fiddle sharp,
Winds the French horn, and twangs the tingling
    harp;
Till, like great Jove, the leader, figuring in,
Attunes to order the chaotic din.


Now all seems hush'd; but no, one fiddle will
Give, half-ashamed, a tiny flourish still.
Foil'd in his crash, the leader of the clan
Reproves with frowns the dilatory man:
Then on his candlestick thrice taps his bow,
Nods a new signal, and away they go.


Perchance, while pit and gallery cry 'Hats off!'
And awed Consumption checks his chided cough,
Some giggling daughter of the Queen of Love
Drops, reft of pin, her play-bill from above;
Like Icarus, while laughing galleries clap,
Soars, ducks, and dives in air the printed scrap;
But, wiser far than he, combustion fears,
And, as it flies, eludes the chandeliers;
Till, sinking gradual, with repeated twirl,
It settles, curling, on a fiddler's curl,
Who from his powder'd pate, the intruder strikes,
And, for mere malice, sticks it on the spikes.

Say, why these Babel strains from Babel tongues?
Who's that calls 'Silence!' with such leathern lungs?
He who, in quest of quiet, 'Silence!' hoots,
Is apt to make the hubbub he imputes.


What various swains our motley walls contain!—
Fashion from Moorfields, honour from Chick Lane;
Bankers from Paper Buildings here resort,
Bankrupts from Golden Square and Riches Court;
From the Haymarket canting rogues in grain,
Gulls from the Poultry, sots from Water Lane;
The Lottery-cormorant, the auction shark,
The full-price master, and the half-price clerk;
Boys who long linger at the gallery-door,
With pence twice five—they want but twopence
    more;
Till some Samaritan the twopence spares,
And sends them jumping up the gallery-stairs.


Critics we boast who ne'er their malice balk,
But talk their minds—we wish they'd mind their
    talk;
Big-worded bullies, who by quarrels live—
Who give the lie, and tell the lie they give;
Jews from St. Mary Axe, for jobs so wary,
That for old clothes they'd even axe St. Mary;
And bucks with pockets empty as their pate,
Lax in their gaiters, laxer in their gait;
Who oft, when we our house lock up, carouse
With tippling tipstaves in a lock-up house. . . .

JAMES SMITH

In October 1812 *the above poem, the last quarter of which has been omitted here, was published by James & Horace Smith as one of the supposed Rejected Addresses, sent in but not selected for reading on the first night of the reopening of Drury Lane Theatre. Lord Byron and Lord Jeffrey praised them, and the latter said of this one: "The Theatre", by the Rev. G. Crabbe, we rather think is the best piece in the collection. It is an exquisite and most masterly imitation not only of the peculiar style, but of the taste, temper, and manner of description of that most original author.'*

*The following punning verses on Surnames were also written by James Smith.*

## SURNAMES

Men once were surnamed for their shape or estate
    (You all may from history worm it),
There was Louis the bulky, and Henry the Great,
    John Lackland, and Peter the Hermit:
But now, when the doorplates of misters and dames
    Are read, each so constantly varies,
From the owner's trade figure, and calling surnames
    Seem given by the rule of contraries.

Mr. Wise is a dunce, Mr. King is a whig,
    Mr. Coffin's uncommonly sprightly,
And huge Mr. Little broke down in a gig
    While driving fat Mrs. Golightly.
At Bath, where the feeble go more than the stout
    (A conduct well worthy of Nero),
Over poor Mr. Lightfoot, confined with the gout,
    Mr. Heavyside danced a bolero.

Miss Joy, wretched maid, when she chose Mr. Love,
　　Found nothing but sorrow await her;
She now holds in wedlock, as true as a dove,
　　That fondest of mates, Mr. Hayter.
Mr. Oldcastle dwells in a modern-built hut;
　　Miss Sage is of madcaps the archest;
Of all the queer bachelors Cupid e'er cut,
　　Old Mr. Younghusband's the starchest.


Mr. Child, in a passion, knock'd down Mr. Rock;
　　Mr. Stone like an aspen-leaf shivers;
Miss Pool used to dance, but she stands like a stock
　　Ever since she became Mrs. Rivers.
Mr. Swift hobbles onward, no mortal knows how,
　　He moves as though cords had entwined him;
Mr. Metcalf ran off upon meeting a cow,
　　With pale Mr. Turnbull behind him.


Mr. Barker's as mute as a fish in the sea,
　　Mr. Miles never moves on a journey,
Mr. Gotobed sits up till half after three,
　　Mr. Makepeace was bred an attorney,
Mr. Gardner can't tell a flower from a root,
　　Mr. Wild with timidity draws back,
Mr. Ryder performs all his journeys on foot,
　　Mr. Foot all his journeys on horseback.


Mr. Penny, whose father was rolling in wealth,
　　Consumed all the fortune his dad won;
Large Mr. LeFever's the picture of health;
　　Mr. Goodenough is but a bad one;

Mr. Cruikshank stept into three thousand a year
  By showing his leg to an heiress:
Now I hope you'll acknowledge I've made it quite clear
  Surnames ever go by contraries.

JAMES SMITH

Lines from

## THE AMATEUR ORLANDO

The night has come; the house is packed
  From pit to gallery;
As those who through the curtain peep
  Quake inwardly to see.
  A squeak is in the orchestra,
  The leader draws across
Th' intestines of the agile cat
  The tail of the noble hoss.

GEORGE T. LANIGAN

## TRADITIONAL RHYME ON THE VALE OF AVON PLACE-NAMES

Piping Pebworth, Dancing Marston,
Haunted Hillborough, Hungry Grafton,
Dodging Exhall, Papist Wixford,
Beggarly Broom, and Drunken Bidford.

## BY WINDRUSH, THAMES AND EVENLODE

What word-magician, more than man,
Silvanus, Faunus, Aegipan,
Or poet-godsire, unavowed,
Nameless himself, his haunts endowed

[228]

With names, delicious, quaint or queer
That sound like music in the ear
Of travellers who take the road
By Windrush, Thames and Evenlode?
I'd be contented with a hovel
At Ambrosden or Minster Lovell
Far from the flutters and the flicks,
A nook at Noke, a box at Bix.
I often ponder which would suit
Best of the Baldons, Marsh or Toot.
From Adderbury one could hop
To Adwell or to Addlestrop;
From Heythrop, Hook and Chipping Norton
There's all the Cotswolds to cavort on.
Though I aspire, when feeling lordly,
To Chastleton or Stratton Audley,
I'd be resigned to something smaller
At Filkins, Faringdon or Fawler.
At other times I set my heart on
Ewelme or Wychwood or Tadmarton
Or Duns or Great or Little Tew.
I wonder was it ever true
That folks at Oddington were *fou*?
Did men and cows at Cuddesdon chew
The cud? Was Horspath closed to cars?
Was Shotover a seat of Mars?
Seeking for slumber, one would not
Choose Nettlebed or Clattercot;
At Easington we'd sleep like logs,
And snore like pigs at Broughton Poggs.
How good to spend a summer's day
At Hampton Poyle and Hampton Gay,
Or fade and leave the world unseen

At Coombe or Weston-on-the-Green!
How sweet at Swerford-on-the-Swere
To linger for at least a year,
Or list the lazy waters lap
By Bablockhythe or Goring Gap,
Or, free from frenzy, fleet the time,
Glamoured at Glympton-on-the-Glyme!

A. H. VERNÈDE

## LINES FROM SALLY BROWN

His death, which happen'd in his berth,
    At forty-odd befell:
They went and told the sexton, and
    The sexton toll'd the bell.

THOMAS HOOD: 1799–1845

## THE WRITER

Titus reads neither prose nor rhyme;
He writes himself; he has no time.

HILDEBRAND JACOB: 1693–1739

## THE HIGHBROW

For learned nonsense has a deeper sound
Than easy sense, and goes for more profound.

SAMUEL BUTLER

*Upon the Abuse of Human Learning*

## THE BROKEN DISH

What's life but full of care and doubt,
  With all its fine humanities;
With parasols we walk about,
  Long pigtails and such vanities.

We plant pomegranate trees and things,
  And go in gardens sporting,
With toys and fans of peacocks' wings,
  To painted ladies courting.

We gather flowers of every hue,
  And fish in boats for fishes,
Build summer-houses painted blue—
  But life's as frail as dishes.

Walking about their grove of trees,
  Blue bridges and blue rivers,
How little thought them two Chinese
  They'd both be smashed to shivers.

THOMAS HOOD

## PRIVY GRAFFITI
### FROM A WALL IN ITALY

*A certain distinguished English gentleman on his return from a
holiday in Italy remarked that though he could not speak the language he was convinced that the Italians were a nation of poets, for
they often had a little rhyme (which he had copied down) put up in
their cloakrooms. Thus:*

Sotto il lavabo
Si trova uno vaso.

*The interpretation of this 'rhyme', which he discovered later, read:*

Underneath the basin
Will be found a pot!

## PRIVY GRAFFITI
### FROM A WALL IN PARIS

Les noms des fous
Sont écrits partout.

*The names of fools are written everywhere.*

## FINAL WHIMSIES

In a wife I would desire
What in whores is always found
The lineaments of gratified desire.

WILLIAM BLAKE

' 'Tis not her coldness, father,
That chills my labouring breast;
It's that confounded cucumber
I've ate and can't digest.'

R. H. BARHAM: 1788-1845

*R. H. Barham was the author of the celebrated Ingoldsby Legends.*

When I had my operation I displayed a lot of guts,
I could take it, smile, and like it, but the bed-pan
drove me nuts.

ANON

# Old School Books, Samplers, Sundials, Bells, With Wise-Saw Jingles Weave Their Spells.

★ ★ ★ ★ ★ ★ ★ ★ ★ ★ ★ ★ ★ ★ ★ ★ ★ ★ ★ ★ ★

*Among certain minor family treasures there is an old sampler which bears the legend: 'Jane Milsom her work at A. Bennetts School aged 7 Years'.*

*Stiffly stitched lettering, set within embroidered borders, where a bonneted spinster with parasol and reticule poses primly amid nosegays of many colours before a square red wool house, admonishes the young in these words:*

> Lord what is life: 'Tis like a flower,
>     That blossoms, and is gone!
> We see it flourish for an hour,
>     With all its beauty on:
> But Death comes like a wintry day,
> And cuts the pretty flower away.

*All the more reason, then, that we should enjoy life while it lasts, as the authors of most of the rhymes in this chapter advise. From the Far East too comes this same advice. As Lin Yutang says, in his beautiful book,* My Country and My People:

'For the Chinese the end of life lies not in life after death, for the idea that we live in order to die, as taught by Christianity, is incomprehensible; nor in Nirvana, for that is too metaphysical; nor in the satisfaction of accomplishment, for that is

too vainglorious; nor yet in progress for progress' sake, for
that is meaningless. The true end, the Chinese have decided in
a singularly clear manner, lies in the enjoyment of a simple
life, especially the family life, and in harmonious social rela-
tionships. The first poem that a child learns in school runs:

> While soft clouds by warm breezes are wafted in the morn,
> Lured by flowers, past the river I roam on and on.
> They'll say, "Look at that old man on a spree!"
> And know not that my spirit's on happiness borne. . . .

'The difference between China and the West seems to be
that the Westerners have a greater capacity for getting and
making more things and a lesser ability to enjoy them, while
the Chinese have a greater determination and capacity to
enjoy the few things they have. This trait, our concentration
on earthly happiness, is as much a result as a cause of the ab-
sence of religion. For if one cannot believe in the life hereafter
as the consummation of the present life, one is forced to make
the most of this life before the farce is over. . . .

'The end of all knowledge is to serve human happiness.'

> Lord, what is Life? 'Tis like a flower
> That blossoms, and is gone . . .

*And so we should say with that jolly old parson, Robert Herrick:*

> Gather ye rosebuds while ye may,
> Old Time is still a-flying,
> And he that will not while he may,
> To-morrow will be sighing.

*It was this same hilarious and ever halcyon cleric, Herrick, who
wrote 'A Ternarie of Littles, upon a Pipkin of Jellie Sent to a Lady',
of which the last verses run:*

A little Streame best fits a little Boat;
A little lead best fits a little Float;
As my small Pipe best fits my little Note.

A little meat best fits a little bellie,
As sweetly, Lady, give me leave to tell ye,
This little pipkin fits this little Jellie.

ROBERT HERRICK: 1591–1674

*But the Cornish lad did not agree with the suggestion about a little bellie—and so:*

There was a young lad of St. Just
Who ate apple pie till he bust;
It wasn't the fru-it
That caused him to do it,
What finished him off was the crust.

ANON

*That puncture recalls the old schoolboy Punctuation Puzzle:*

Caesar entered on his head
A helmet on each foot
A sandal in his hand he had
His trusty sword to boot.

Founded on a Ballad

## 'THE LAMENTATION OF A BAD MARKET: OR THE DROWNDING OF THREE CHILDREN IN THE THAMES' (1653)

Three children sliding on the ice,
Upon a summer's day,
As it fell out, they all fell in,
The rest they ran away.          ANON

[235]

## PARODY ON THE NURSERY RHYME 'MARY'S LITTLE LAMB' BY SARAH JOSEPHA HALE (1788–1879)

Mary had a little lamb,
She ate it with mint sauce,
And everywhere that Mary went
The lamb went too, of course.

ANON

## ANOTHER PARODY

Mary had a little bear
To which she was so kind
That everywhere dear Mary went
You saw her bear running along beside her.

ANON

*The following anonymous rhyme was seen on a poster carried by protesting housewives amongst the crowd demonstrating near the House of Commons during the debate on Winston Churchill's Censure Motion against the Labour Government for its mishandling of the meat situation and the reduction of the meat ration to the lowest level in history: February 1951.*

Mary had a little lamb,
But her sister came to grief
She lived in 1951
And only got Corned Beef.

## AMERICAN PARODY

Mary had a little lamb
Whose fleece was white as snow;

[236]

She took it down to Pittsburgh
And look at the dam thing now!

ANON

## ADDENDUM TO THE TEN COMMANDMENTS

Thou shalt not covet thy neighbour's wife,
Nor the ox her husband bought her;
But thank the Lord you're not forbidden
To covet your neighbour's daughter.

ANON

## NO GRACE BEFORE MEAT

Does any man of common sense
Think ham and eggs give God offence?
Or that a herring has a charm
The Almighty's anger to disarm?
Wrapped in His majesty divine,
D'you think He cares on what we dine?

DEAN SWIFT

## SCRIBBLED ON FLY-LEAVES IN OLD SCHOOL BOOKS

If you this precious volume bone
Jack Ketch will get you for his own.

Black is the raven
Black is the rook
But Blacker the Sinner
That pinches this book.

[237]

This book is mine
This boot another
Touch not the one
For fear of the other.

He what takes what isn't his'n
When he's cotched will go to prison.

ALL TRADITIONAL, FROM PUBLIC SCHOOLS

## INSCRIPTION ON AN OLD BELL

I mean to make it understood
That though I'm little I am good.

FROM GREAT BADDOW: 1781

## TWO INSCRIPTIONS FROM OLD SUNDIALS

Life's but a shade: man is but dust;
The dyall sayes *dyall* we must.

Time wastes our bodies and our wits;
But we waste Time, so we are quits.

## QUINCTILIAN

Quinctilian enjoyed the quince-buds
(which he couldn't distinguish from peach):
He was brooding on asyndeton, astyanax
And other figures of speech! . . .

AUTHOR UNKNOWN

*From Edith Sitwell's 'Look! The Sun'*

[238]

## SPRING

Spring, the sweet spring, is the year's pleasant king;
Then blooms each thing, then maids dance in a ring,
Cold doth not sting, the pretty birds do sing—
  Cuckoo, jug-jug, pu-we, to-witta-woo!

The palm and may make country houses gay,
Lambs frisk and play, the shepherds pipe all day,
And we hear ay birds tune this merry lay—
  Cuckoo, jug-jug, pu-we, to-witta-woo!

The fields breathe sweet, the daisies kiss our feet,
Young lovers meet, old wives a-sunning sit,
In every street these tunes our ears do greet—
  Cuckoo, jug-jug, pu-we, to-witta-woo!

THOMAS NASHE: 1567–1601


## AMBITION

Get place and wealth; if possible, with grace;
If not, by any means get wealth and place.

POPE


## IF ALL THE WORLD WERE PAPER

If all the world were paper,
And all the sea were inke;
And all the trees were bread and cheese,
What should we do for drinke?

ANON: SEVENTEENTH CENTURY

## POETIC THOUGHT

Oh Moon! when I look on thy beautiful face,
Careering along through the boundaries of space,
The thought has quite frequently come to my mind,
If ever I'll gaze on thy glorious behind.

**A HOUSEMAID POET**

*Said to have been written by Edmund Gosse's serving maid,
found in her mattress after her death.*

## ? THE SCHOOLBOY

His speech was yet as halting as his gait,
Only less brutish than his moral state.

**ANON**

## SEE, WILLIE! SEE 'ER GO!

Civile, si ergo,
Fortibus es in ero.
Gnoses mare, Thebe trux.
Vatis inem?
Causan dux!

**ANON**

## LITTLE WILLIE

Little Willie from his mirror
Licked the mercury right off,
Thinking, in his childish error,
It would cure the whooping cough.

At the funeral his mother
Brightly said to Mrs. Brown:

' 'Twas a chilly day for Willie
When the mercury went down!'

ANON

## LOVEY-DOVEY

Poets call the dove
The symbol of pure love;
But have you heard the things they do?
COO!

HAROLD MORLAND

# Nursery Rhymes

## DOCTOR BELL

Doctor Bell fell down the well
And broke his collar-bone.
Doctors should attend the sick
And leave the well alone.

(?) EIGHTEENTH CENTURY

## FLEET FLIGHT

A flea met a fly in a flue,
Said the flea let us fly
Said the fly let us flee
So they flew through a flaw in the flue.

NINETEENTH CENTURY

### FLIGHTY FLEAS

An odd little thing is a flea
You can't tell a he from a she
But he can, and she can——
Whoopee!

TWENTIETH CENTURY

### ABEY! SEE D' GOLDFISH?

A.B.C.D. Gol'fish?
M.N.O. Gol'fish.
S.D.R. Gol'fish.
R.D.R. Gol'fish!

YIDDISH

### ULTRA-MODERN NURSERY RHYME

Hush-a-bye, baby, your milk's in the tin,
Mummy has got you a nice sitter-in;
Hush-a-bye, baby, now don't get a twinge
While Mummy and Daddy are out on the binge.

AUTHOR UNTRACED

### PERSONAL HYGIENE FOR PUSSIES

Ding dong bell
Pussie's in the well
But now we've put some Izal down
And never mind the smell!

ANON

# Toasting the Ladies

## AN OLD TOAST

Here's to the love that lies in Woman's eyes,
And lies and lies and lies and lies and LIES!

ANON

## ANOTHER FOR MOTHER

Here's to the happiest days of my life,
Spent in the arms of another man's wife—
My mother!

ANON

## A NEW TOAST

Here's to Lying Lips,
Though lying lips are bores,
But lying lips are mighty sweet
When they lie next to yours!

ANON

# Queer People
## He on Him and Her: She on Her and Him
## In Jingle, Verse, and Prayer, or Epitaph
## and Hymn

★ ★ ★ ★ ★ ★ ★ ★ ★ ★ ★ ★ ★ ★ ★ ★ ★ ★ ★ ★

*Below are given Charles Leland's theories on the origin of the word 'Masher'—with his verses about one.*

*These will serve to introduce other, even queerer, 'Queer People'.*

### THE MASHER

*The word to 'mash' in the sense of causing love or attracting by a glance or fascinating look, came into ordinary slang from the American stage. Thus an actress was often fined for 'mashing' or smiling at men in the audience. It was introduced by the well-known gipsy family of actors, C., among whom Romany was habitually spoken. The word 'masher' or 'mash' means in that tongue to allure, delude, or entice. It was doubtless much aided in its popularity by its quasi-identity with the English word. A girl could be called a masher as she could be called a man-killer, or killing. But there can be no doubt as to the gipsy origin of 'mash' as used on the stage. I am indebted for this information to the late well-known impresario Palmer of New York, and I made a note of it years before the term had become popular.*

It was in the Indian summer-time, when life is tender brown,
And people in the country talk of going into town,
When the nights are crisp and cooling, though the sun is warm
    by day,
In the home-like town of Glasgow, in the State of Iowa;

It was in the railroad deepô of that greatly-favoured zone,
That a young man met a stranger, who was still not all un-
    known,
For they had run-countered casual in riding in the car,
And the latter to the previous had offered a cigar.

Now as the primal gentleman was nominated Gale,
It follows that the secondary man was Mr. Dale;
This is called poetic justice when arrangements fit in time,
And Fate allows the titles to accommodate in rhyme.

And a lovely sense of autumn seemed to warble in the air;
Boys with baskets selling peaches were vibratin' everywhere,
While in the mellow distance folks were gettin' in their corn,
And the biggest yellow punkins ever seen since you were born.

Now a gradual sensation emotioned this our Gale,
That he'd seldom seen so fine a man for cheek as Mr. Dale;
Yet simultaneous he felt that he was all the while
The biggest dude and cock-a-hoop within a hundred mile.

For the usual expression of his quite enormous eyes
Was that of two ripe gooseberries who've been decreed a
    prize;
Like a goose apart from berries, too—though not removed
    from sauce—
He conversed on lovely Woman as if he were all her boss.

[245]

Till, in fact, he stated plainly that, between his face and cash,
There was not a lady living whom he was not sure to mash;
The wealthiest, the loveliest, of families sublime,
At just a single look from him must all give in in time.

Now when our Dale had got along so far upon this strain,
They saw a Dream of Loveliness descending from the train,
A proud and queenly beauty of a transcendental face,
With gloves unto her shoulders, and the most expensive lace.

All Baltimore and New Orleans seemed centred into one,
As if their stars of beauty had been fused into a sun;
But, oh! her frosty dignity expressed a kind of glow
Like sunshine when thermometers show thirty grades below.

But it flashed a gleam of shrewdness into the head of Gale,
And with aggravatin' humour he exclaimed to Mr. Dale,
'Since every girl's a cricket-ball and you're the only bat,
If you want to show you're champion, go in and mash on that.

'I will bet a thousand dollars, and plank them on the rub,
That if you try it thither, you will catch a lofty snub.
I don't mean but what a lady may reply to what you say,
But I bet you cannot win her into wedding in a day.'

A singular emotion enveloped Mr. Dale;
One would say he seemed confuseled, for his countenance was
    pale:
At first there came an angry look, and when that look did get,
He larft a wild and hollow larf, and said, 'I take the debt.'

'The brave deserve the lovely—every woman may be won;
What men have fixed before us may by other men be done.

You will lose your thousand dollars. For the first time in my
   life
I have gazed upon a woman whom I wish to make my wife.'

Like a terrier at a rabbit, with his hat upon his eyes,
Mr. Dale, the awful masher, went head-longing at the prize,
Looking rather like a party simply bent to break the peace.
Mr. Gale, with smiles, expected just a yell for the police.

Oh! what are women made of? Oh! what can women be?
From Eves to Jersey Lilies what bewildering sights we see!
One listened on the instant to all the Serpent said;
The other paid attention right away to Floral Ned.

With a blow as with a hammer the intruder broke the ice,
And the proud and queenly beauty seemed to think it awful
   nice.
Mr. Gale, as he beheld it, with a trembling heart began
To realize he really was a most astonished man.

Shall I tell you how he wooed her? Shall I tell you how he won?
How they had a hasty wedding ere the evening was done?
For when all things were considered, the fond couple thought
   it best—
Such things are not uncommon in the wild and rapid West.

Dale obtained the thousand dollars, and then vanished with
   the dream.
Gale stayed in town with sorrow, like a spoon behind the
   cream,
Till one morning in the paper he read, though not in rhymes,
How a certain blooming couple had been married fifty times!

How they wandered o'er the country, how the bridegroom
    used to bet
He would wed the girl that evening—how he always pulled
    the debt;
How his eyes were large and greensome; how, in fact, to end
    the tale,
Their very latest victim was a fine young man named Gale!

CHARLES G. LELAND

## THE COMMUNIST

What is a Communist? One who has yearnings
To share equal profits from unequal earnings
Be he idler or bungler or both, he is willing
To fork out his sixpence and pocket your shilling.

EBENEZER ELLIOTT: 1781–1849

## EPIGRAM FROM THE FRENCH

Sir, I admit your general rule,
That every poet is a fool:
But you yourself may serve to show it,
That every fool is not a poet.

ALEXANDER POPE

## THE HONEST DEALER

All of us know that money talks throughout our glorious
    nation;
But money whispers low compared to business reputation;
Pull off no slick nor crooked deal, for pennies or for dollars—
God! Think of all the trade you'll lose if just one sucker
    hollers!

ANON

## ON MODERN CRITICS

For daring nonsense seldom fails to hit,
Like scattered shot, and pass with some for wit.

SAMUEL BUTLER

## INHUMANITY

Man's inhumanity to man is hard,
In fact, 'tis scarce in line with aught that's human;
And yet—'tis quite angelic, as compared
With woman's inhumanity to woman.

ANON

## HERESY

*Lines written after the trial for heresy of the Bishop
Colenso of Natal, nearly a hundred years ago*

THE ARCHBISHOP:

My dear Colenso, with regret,
We hierarchs in conclave met,
Beg you, you most disturbing writer,
To take off your colonial mitre;
This course we urge upon you strongly:
Believe me, yours most truly, LONGLEY.

THE BISHOP:

My dear Archbishop, to resign
This Zulu diocese of mine,
And own myself a heathen dark,
Because I've doubts of Noah's Ark,
And think it right to tell men so—
Is *not* the course for, COLENSO.

ANON

## ON THE TRIUMPH OF RATIONALISM

When Reason's ray shines over all
And puts the Saints to rout,
Then Peter's holiness will pall
And Paul's will peter out.

CANON ALFRED AINGER: 1837–1904

## GASBAGS

I'm thankful that the sun and moon
Are both hung up so high
That no pretentious hand can stretch
And pull them from the sky.
If they were not, I have no doubt,
But some reforming ass
Would recommend to take them down
And light the world with gas.

ANON: NINETEENTH CENTURY

## BEG, BORROW OR SQUEAL

'Tis a very good world to live in,
To lend, or to spend, or to give in;
But to beg or to borrow, or get a man's own,
'Tis the very worst world that ever was known.

ATTRIBUTED TO THE EARL OF ROCHESTER

## THE TESTIMONIAL

He has asked my support, which I own I regret,
And my mind is not wholly made up:
For it's ticklish to find a good home for a pet
And not sell the public a pup.

A. & K. FARRER

[250]

## THE BLOODY ORKNEYS

This bloody town's a bloody cuss—
No bloody trains, no bloody bus,
And no one cares for bloody us—
      In bloody Orkney.

The bloody roads are bloody bad,
The bloody folks are bloody mad,
They'd make the brightest bloody sad,
      In bloody Orkney.

All bloody clouds, and bloody rains,
No bloody kerbs, no bloody drains,
The Council's got no bloody brains,
      In bloody Orkney.

Everything's so bloody dear,
A bloody bob, for bloody beer,
And is it good?—no bloody fear,
      In bloody Orkney.

The bloody 'flicks' are bloody old,
The bloody seats are bloody cold,
You can't get in for bloody gold
      In bloody Orkney.

The bloody dances make you smile
The bloody band is bloody vile,
It only cramps your bloody style,
      In bloody Orkney.

No bloody sport, no bloody games,
No bloody fun, the bloody dames
Won't even give their bloody names
    In bloody Orkney.

Best bloody place is bloody bed,
With bloody ice on bloody head,
You might as well be bloody dead,
    In bloody Orkney.

**CAPTAIN HAMISH BLAIR**

## RELIGION

Those petulant capricious sects,
The maggots of corrupted texts. . . .

**SAMUEL BUTLER**

## THE HYMN OF THE OLD SECT OF THE MUGGLETONIANS

I do believe in God alone,
Likewise in Reeve and Muggleton.
This is the God which we believe;
None salvation-knowledge hath
But those of Muggleton and Reeve.
Christ is the Muggletonian's King,
With whom eternally they'll sing.

**TRADITIONAL**

*Sung for 200 years and more*

## HYMNS A. & M.

*By way of contrast, less than a hundred years ago church congregations were still fervently singing:*

> Take my silver and my gold,
> Not a mite will I withhold!

*But they followed this up with the 'pawnbroking hymn':*

> Whatever, Lord, we lend to Thee
> Repaid a thousandfold will be.
> Then gladly will we lend to Thee!

*Their reward was awaiting them in Heaven! And why not?
They had not much hope of reward on Earth. They had been well
and truly trained not to be covetous or envious:*

> Oh, let us love our own vocations.
> Bless the squire and his relations
> And always know our proper stations!

### EPIGRAM:

*On seeing the words Domus Ultima over a vault
for the Duke of Richmond's family*

> Did he, who first inscrib'd this wall
> Not read, or not believe St. Paul,
> Who says that far above there stands
> Another House, not made with hands.
>
> Or may we gather from these words
> That House is not a House of Lords?

WILLIAM CLARKE

# More Lines from Hymns

### GYMNASTIC SERAPHS

Let high-born Seraphs tune the lyre,
  And, as they tune it, fall
Before His face who formed their choir,
  And crown Him Lord of all!
*Lines from 'All hail the power of Jesus' Name'*

### FUSSY FATHERS

Fathers themselves are God's children,
Keep them still!

### MOTHER AND THE CHILD SHE-BEAR

Can a woman's tender care
Cease toward the child she bare?

### SATAN'S NURSLING?

Satan trembles when he sees
The weakest saint upon his knees.

### SAMUEL THE JEW-BOY

His watch the temple child,
the little Levite, kept.[1]

### PSEUDO-HYMN

If I were a Cassowary
On the plains of Timbuctoo,

---

[1] The old man meek and mild,
The priest of Israel, slept!

I would eat a missionary,
Coat and bands and hymn-book too.

ATTRIBUTED TO BISHOP SAMUEL WILBERFORCE

## HYMN AND PRAYER FOR CIVIL SERVANTS

O, Lord, Grant that this day we come to no decisions, neither run we into any kind of responsibility, but that all our doings may be ordered to establish new departments, for ever and ever. Amen.

O Thou who seest all things below,
Grant that Thy servants may go slow,
That they may study to comply
With regulations till they die.

Teach us, O Lord, to reverence
Committees more than common sense;
To train our minds to make no plan
And pass the baby when we can.

So when the tempter seeks to give
Us feelings of initiative,
Or when alone we go too far,
Chastise us with a circular.

Mid war and tumult, fire and storms,
Give strength O Lord, to deal out forms.
Thus may Thy servants ever be
A flock of perfect sheep for Thee.

*Published anonymously in the*
*'Daily Telegraph'*

*A few more lines from actual hymns will show the fatal superiority of the pseudo-hymn writer to his professional colleague—not only in versification but also in a grasp of reality.*

## THE POOR WORM PANTS

Pardon a worm that would draw near,
That would to Thee his heart resign;
A worm by self and sin opprest,
That pants to reach the promised rest!

*Kemble's 'Psalms and Hymns', No. 349, Verse 1*

*An old child-puzzler from another hymn was:*
Gladly, the cross-eyed bear!

## THE HEBREWS

How odd of God
To choose the Jews.

W. N. EWER

But not so odd,
As those who choose
A Jewish God,
Yet spurn the Jews.

CECIL BROWNE

Dear Mr. Browne,
Don't you confuse
Jehovah with the Jesus whose
Own people spurned Him?—
Why enthuse?
So cordially,
H. E. B. REWS.

ARD SLOK

## THE PRE-RAPHAELITE

A Pre-Raphaelite
Had to have things right.
The patient redhead, Elizabeth Siddal,
Lay in the bathtub up to her middle
(But richly gowned)
To show what she would look like drowned.
At last she sneezed: Oh Mr. Millais,
Do I 'ave to welter 'ere all day?
It's enough to congeal ya:
Posing for Ophelia.

CHRISTOPHER MORLEY

*Quoted from 'Mandarin in Manhattan', Lippincott, New York, 1933. (First published by Faber & Faber.)*

## THE IMPERFECT ARTIST

Good Mr. Fortune, A.R.A.,
Rejoiced in twenty sons,
But even there he failed, they say,
To get a likeness once.

GEORGE ROSTREVOR HAMILTON
*From 'Lucilius'*

## THE SURREALIST

Though art be on vacation,
    The studio remains;
The well of inspiration
    Is backing out of drains.

Come, let us daub, my crazys,
    Surrealize the thrill
Of soapsuds on the daisies
    And skylarks in the swill.

Ours not to reason whether
    Surprise surpasseth wonder,
When man hath joined together
    What God hath rent asunder.

LEONARD FEENEY, S.J.

*Quoted from Father Feeney's poem in his volume of essays
entitled 'Survival till Seventeen' (p. 100), Sheed & Ward,
London, 1942.*

[258]

## THE ARTIST

The Artist and his Luckless Wife
They lead a horrid haunted life,
Surrounded by the things he's made
That are not wanted by the trade.

The world is very fair to see;
The Artist will not let it be;
He fiddles with the works of God,
And makes them look uncommon odd.

The Artist is an awful man,
He does not do the things he can;
He does the things he cannot do,
And we attend the private view.

The Artist uses honest paint
To represent things as they ain't,
He then asks money for the time
It took to perpetrate the crime.

SIR WALTER RALEIGH

*Captain H.M. Raleigh, son of the late Sir Walter Raleigh, has told me that 'The Artist' originally appeared in* Laughter from a Cloud, *a collection, published not long after the author's death in 1922, in a limited edition, by Constable. The collection was made by Captain Raleigh from his father's writings. 'The poem itself was written, verse by verse, on postcards, and sent by my father to his friend Robert Anning Bell, R.A. It was, in fact, one end of a correspondence. Unhappily we have never been able to trace the replies sent by the artist himself!'*

## GOD AND THE SOLDIER

*The original quatrain (from which the following still popular verse was adapted, substituting 'soldier' for 'doctor') was written by Euricius Cordus (1486–1535), the poet and physician, whose son Valerius compiled what is said to be the first official pharmacopoeia—The Nuremberg Dispensatorium.*

> God and the soldier we alike adore,
> When on the brink of danger, not before;
> The danger past, both are alike requited,
> God is forgotten and the soldier slighted.

## THE CRIME

> On the First of September, one Sunday morn,
> I shot a hen pheasant in standing corn
> Without a licence. Contrive who can
> Such a cluster of crimes against God and man!

RICHARD MONCKTON, 1ST LORD HOUGHTON

## FAULTS, MALE AND FEMALE

Men they may have many faults
But women only two—
Everything they say
And everything they do.

ANON

## NOT CRICKET

*George Giffen, the greatest all-round cricketer in Australian history, was accused of using undue influence to ensure the inclusion of his not-so-good brother, Walter, in the team which came to England in 1893. The following lines are a part of the comment in verse which appeared in a contemporary issue of the* Sydney Bulletin:

What boots it if, before attack
Of English foes, our fellows falter?
I am the great Australian crack,
And love my little brother Walter.

If I should take the trip and 'tin'
And leave him, I'd deserve a halter:
And I'll be hanged if I join in
If they pass over little Walter.

ANON

*N.B. Walter went, but did not play in the tests!*

## THE PERFECT MARRIAGE

I would be married, but I'd have no wife,
I would be married to a single life.

RICHARD CRASHAW

## NOT SO GAY

One wife is too much for one husband to hear
But two at a time there's no mortal can bear.

JOHN GAY

## ANOTHER MATRIMONIAL THOUGHT

In the blithe days of honeymoon,
With Kate's allurements smitten,
I lov'd her late, I lov'd her soon,
And call'd her dearest kitten.

But now my kitten's grown a cat,
And cross like other wives,
O! by my soul, my honest Matt,
I fear she has nine lives.

JAMES BOSWELL

## BAD WOMEN

Oh the gladness of a woman when she's glad!
And oh the sadness of a woman when she's sad!
  But the gladness of her gladness
  And the sadness of her sadness
Are as nothing to her badness when she's bad!

ANON

## CONSCIENCE

King David and King Solomon led merry, merry lives,
With many, many lady friends and many, many wives,

But when old age crept over them, with many, many
    qualms,
King Solomon wrote Proverbs and King David wrote the
    Psalms.

DR. JAMES BALL NAYLOR: U.S.A. (born 1860)

## THE YOUNG METAPHYSICIAN

There once was a metaphysician
Who claimed that he didn't exist,
But when he explained his position
They exclaimed, 'Well, you'll never be missed!'

ANON

## A FRIEND OF YOURS?

He comes, but not with clamorous gush,
Nor with defiant, echoing rush;
With voiceless footfall on the floor,
He comes to stay—the bore, the bore!

Soft is his voice as unbaked bread,
And softer than his voice, his head;
His talk is flatter than the floor,
But yet he stays—the bore, the bore!

ROBERT J. BURDETTE

## THE GOOD AND THE CLEVER

If only the good were the clever,
    If only the clever were good,
The world would be better than ever
    We thought that it possibly could.

[263]

But, alas, it is seldom or never
    That either behave as they should;
For the good are so harsh to the clever,
    The clever so rude to the good.

ATTRIBUTED TO ELIZABETH WORDSWORTH:
1840–1932

*Latin version*

Si callidus vir quisquis est fiat probus,
    probive fiant callide,
beata certe vita, qualem vix adhuc
    quisquam futuram credidit.
nunc raro fiunt, immo non umquam, nefas,
    neque hi neque illi quod decet.
nam callidus vir quisquis est, rodunt probi,
    probosque ridet callidus.

J. B. POYNTON

# Backward-Foreword with Acknowledgments

★ ★ ★ ★ ★ ★ ★ ★ ★ ★ ★ ★ ★ ★ ★ ★ ★ ★ ★ ★ ★ ★

In addition to those to whom this book is dedicated I wish to thank a great number of generous contributors who, over a long period of years and in many different parts of the world, have given—and are still giving me—Verse and Worse!

My gratitude goes out also to numerous other helpers who have most kindly assisted me in diverse ways to compile this collection. Without their constant interest and practical good will many of the original and unpublished poems printed here would perhaps have remained unpublished, and would gradually have been lost through the lapse of time. I am, therefore, specially grateful for all the help I have received in this enterprise (a hobby most entertaining, though taxing for the collector, but fortunately free from the attentions of the entertainment-tax collector) to recover a rich collection of rhymes from the invisible treasury of tradition and the silent depths of memory.

I have kept notes of known sources for several years and have made diligent search for others which were in doubt. I can but hope that all helpers, including the authors and publishers of the works from which I have been courteously permitted to quote, will find their names recorded in the alphabetical lists which follow:

Mr. Jack Anthony, Mr. K. L. Angus, Mrs. Beatrice Athenogenes, Wing-Commander C. Arthur Barker & Mrs. Diana Barker, Miss Louise Bateman, Miss Edwina Beauchamp, Lord

Berners, Mr. J. Lamorna Birch, R.A., Mr. Henry Boddington, F.R.I.B.A., Mr. Hulme Chadwick, The Right Hon. Winston S. Churchill, P.C., C.H., M.P., His Highness the Maharajah of Cooch Behar, Mr. Arthur Cooper, Mr. Oswald Couldrey, 'V. H. Drummond' (Mrs. A. C. Swetenham) the illustrator of this book, Mr. C. W. Dyson-Smith, Mr. Geoffrey Edwards & the Hon. Mrs. Geoffrey Edwards, the Rev. Dr. Austin Farrer, Father Leonard Feeney, S.J., Mr. B. Fleetwood-Walker, A.R.A., Mr. W. B. Garner, Mr. Charles Graves, the Rev. Dr. L. W. Grensted, Mr. Arthur Griffiths, F.R.I.B.A., Mr. Nathaniel Gubbins, Mr. Rome Guthrie, F.R.I.B.A., Mr. Vernon Hardy, Mr. Will Hay, Jr., Mr. Robin A. Henderson, Mr. F. C. A. Herrmann, Mr. Bruce Hobbs, Mr. C. Randle Jackson, Mr. Michael Jûpe & Mrs. Mary Jûpe, Mr. Cherry Kearton, Mr. Arthur Kidson, Mr. H. L. Kitson, Mr. Collie Knox, Mr. William Martin Larkins, Mr. James Laver, Mr. Ralph Lavers, Mr. John Lee, Mrs. Esmé Lee, Mrs. Robert Longden, Mr. Arnold Lycett, A.R.I.B.A., Brigadier Alan McClare, D.S.O. & Mrs. Frida McClare, Flt.-Lieut. James McGregor & Mrs. Muriel McGregor, Mrs. Dorothy Martin, Mr. H. G. Massey, F.L.A., Chief Librarian, Kensington Public Libraries, Mr. Christopher Morley, Mr. Ernest Newman, Mr. Eric Newton, Mr. Eric Alfred Nicolle, Mr. Billy Payne, Miss Judy Pearson, Mr. Eden Phillpotts, Mr. & Mrs. Michael de Pret-Rouse, Father Hugh Pickles, Miss E. Price, Mr. J. B. Poynton, Lady Raleigh & Captain H. M. Raleigh, Mr. Justin Richardson, Mr. John Ridley, 'Naomi Royde-Smith' (Mrs. Ernest Ditton), Mrs. Agnes Rudie, Mr. Peter F. du Sautoy, Mr. Jack Scott, Mr. Norman Shelley, 'Timothy Shy' (Mr. D. B. Wyndham Lewis), Lieut.-Colonel Vivian Seymer, D.S.O., F.R.I.B.A., Professor T. H. Silcock & Mrs. Margaret Silcock, Mr. & Mrs. Reginald Sinclair, Monsieur André L. Simon, Mr. William Begg Simpson, F.R.I.B.A., Mr. Marshall Sisson,

F.R.I.B.A., Miss Edith Sitwell, Lieut.-Colonel Philip Slessor, Lord Stanley of Alderley, Mr. Stewart Stubbs & Mrs. Jean Stubbs, Major H. Tatham, F.R.I.B.A., Mr. A. H. Vernède, Miss Joan Warren, Mr. John Washburn & Mrs. Mary Ellen Harvey Scott Washburn, Mr. T. R. Whittingham, 'Peter Weir' (Mr. Noel Stafford Robinson), Mrs. Olwen Wilkins, Sir Owen Williams, K.B.E., Group-Captain Frederick Winterbotham, D.S.O., D.F.C., Mr. Geoffrey Wincott, Mr. Ralph Wotherspoon, Captain Alan Young & Mrs. Pamela Young, Mr. Roland Young, Dr. Lin Yutang.

AUTHORS, PUBLISHERS, AND OTHERS THROUGH WHOSE GOOD WILL AND COURTEOUS PERMISSION A NUMBER OF THE POEMS ARE REPRODUCED

Mr. Winston Churchill, who introduced me to a new version of the anonymous verse, 'Fame'. Mrs. Robert Longden, for 'Caligula' & 'Claudius' (not previously published) by the late Dr. Robert Longden. Miss Ruth Silcock for her 'Nell Gwynne' (not previously published) and with gratitude for much other help. The Hon. Mrs. Geoffrey Edwards for her 'The Lives of the Popes' (not previously published). Monsieur André L. Simon, President, the Wine and Food Society, for their permission to quote 'On China Blue' (*Grace During Meat*) by the late Sir Stephen Gaselee. A. M. Heath & Co., Ltd., for permission to quote 'next to of course god' by E. E. Cummings. Macmillan & Co., Ltd., for permission to quote 'The Pazons' and 'I Bended Unto Me' by T. E. Brown. The *Oxford Magazine* and the authors for the following: 'Lay Not Up' by the Rev. Dr. L. W. Grensted; 'The Testimonial' by A. & K. Farrer (the Rev. Dr. & Mrs. Austin Farrer); 'By Windrush, Thames and Evenlode' by A. H. Vernède. The Society of Authors as the Literary Representatives of the Trustees of the Estate of the late A. E. Housman, and Jonathan Cape Ltd., publishers of A. E. Housman's Collected Poems, for one verse from *A.E.H., A Memoir*, by Laurence Housman: 'The Shades of Night' by the late A. E. Housman. The *Observer* (Christmas, 1948) and Robin A. Henderson for his parody 'Ring-a-ring-o'-geranium'. Methuen & Co., Ltd. and R. J. Yeatman and W. C. Sellar for their 'How I Brought the Good News from Aix to Ghent (or Vice-Versa)' from *Horse Nonsense*. Hodder & Stoughton Ltd. and Sir John Squire for his 'If Gray Had Had to Write His Elegy in the Cemetery of Spoon River Instead of in That of Stoke Poges', from *Collected Parodies*. Charles Scribner's Sons for 'A Play on Words', from *Poems* by Eugene Field. D. B. Wyndham Lewis for his 'A Shot at Random', and 'The Lost Chord'; also the *News Chronicle* (11th June 1949) and Timothy Shy (D. B. Wyndham Lewis) in the 'Beyond the Headlines' column, for his 'Jig for Sackbuts'. The *New York Post* and Hughes Mearns for his 'The Lady With Technique' and 'The Perfect Reactionary', and *What Cheer* (Coward-McCann Inc.) by David McCord as my source of these poems. Miss Bridget Muller for her 'Meditation in Autumn', and 'A Fact' (not previously published). Miss Winifred Ambler for her 'Soft Lights and Sweet Music for Psychologists', and 'A Pathetic Psyche' (not previously published), and with gratitude for much other help. Mrs. Hugh Kingsmill for the parody 'The Shropshire Lad' by the late Hugh Kingsmill. The *Tatler* and Justin Richardson for his poems in 'Wholly Matrimony' series (6th and 27th April 1949), 'Wholly Matrimony' and 'Sisters'. The *Evening Standard* (1st February 1949) for 'The Difference Between' (anonymous contributor in the *Londoner's Diary*). Jonathan Cape Ltd. and William Plomer for his 'The Playboy of the Demi-World: 1938', from *The Dorking Thigh*. *What Cheer* (Coward-McCann Inc.) by David McCord, as source for 'The Modern Hiawatha, from *The Song of Milkan-watha* by George Strong. Francis Day & Hunter Ltd. for 'A Rabbit Raced a Turtle', from the song in their Hill-Billy Album No. 1, 'It Ain't Gonna Rain No Mo' '. The *Atlantic Echo* (Azores Force, Services Newspaper) for 'Last Love' by Alexander Silverlock (Arnold Silcock). George Newnes & Co., Ltd. and Ralph Wotherspoon for his 'My Dumb Friends' from *London Opinion* (September 1946). Mr. Arthur Cooper, for introducing me to 'I had a Duck-billed Platypus' reproduced by permission of the proprietors of Punch. Doubleday Doran & Co. and Roland Young, for his The Goat', from *Not for Children*. Eden Phillpotts, for his 'The Wasp'. The Abbey Press, Abingdon, and Oswald Couldrey for his 'Release', from *Triolets and Epigrams*. Angus & Robertson Ltd., Sydney, for 'The Intro', and 'Pilot Cove', from '*The Sentimental Bloke* by the late C. J. Dennis. M. H. Longson for his 'Goings On of an Alter Ego': reproduced by permission of the Proprietors of *Punch* (9th February 1949). Heinemann & Co., Ltd., and Dr. Lin Yutang for the extract from his 'My Country and My People'. Captain Hamish Blair for his 'The Bloody Orkneys' (not previously published) and Mr. Robert Atkinson for introducing the poem to my notice. Faber & Faber Ltd. for 'On the Triumph of Rationalism' by Canon Alfred Ainger, from *The Faber Book of Comic Verse*, and for 'the honey bee' from *archie and mehitabel* by the late Don Marquis. *Good Housekeeping, Canada* for 'The Asterisk' by an anonymous author. Basil Blackwell Ltd., Oxford, and Mr. J. B. Poynton for his Latin version of 'The Good and the Clever' (attributed to Elizabeth Wordsworth) from his *Versions*. Constable & Co., Ltd., and the Trustees of the authors, for 'Good Mr. Fortune A.R.A.' from *Lucilius* by George Rostrevor Hamilton; also for 'The Artist' by Sir Walter Raleigh. Sheed & Ward Ltd. for 'The Surrealist' from

*Survival till Seventeen* by Father Leonard Feeney. S. J. Lippincott & Co., New York, and Faber & Faber Ltd., and Christopher Morley for his 'The Pre-Raphaelite', from *Mandarin
in Manhattan*. The *Sunday Times* (various dates) for a few
quoted hymns and epigrams including 'Epigram on the words
*Domus Ultima*' by the late Mr. William Clarke; discovered in
the Letters to the Editor column. Philpot and C. Lewis Hind
for poems in their 100 *Second Best Poems*: 'Two Men Look
Out' by Frederick Langbridge, and 'The Look' by Sara
Teasdale. *Note,* The copyright of the rhyming chapter titles,
and the poems herein by 'Ard Slok' and 'Incognito', and the
poem 'The Honeymoon Anniversary' (none of which has
been previously published) is owned by their author, Arnold
Silcock.

THE FOLLOWING ARE THE COLLECTIONS TO WHOSE
EDITORS AND PUBLISHERS I AM CHIEFLY, AND GREATLY,
INDEBTED FOR QUOTATIONS

*Pidgin English Sing-Song*, Charles Godfrey Leland (Trübner).
*The Complete Works of C. S. Calverley* (Bell). *The Collected
Poems of T. E. Brown* (Macmillan). *The Faber Book of Comic
Verse*, Michael Roberts (Faber). *The Little Book of American
Humorous Verse* (McKay). *The Book of Humorous Poetry*
(Simpkin). *What Cheer*, David McCord (Coward-McCann).
*Look the Sun!*, Edith Sitwell (Gollancz). *The Pageant of English
Poetry* and *The Collected Poems of Alfred Dennis Godley*
(Oxford). *The Shooting Week-End Book*, Eric Parker (Seeley
Service). *Songs of the Sea and Lays of the Land*, Charles Godfrey
Leland (Black). The poems quoted from the latter and from
*Pidgin English Sing-Song* are reproduced by kind permission
of the publishers who hold the rights (Routledge & Kegan
Paul).

# Index of Authors

WITH THE EXCEPTION OF THOSE WHO STILL REMAIN HIDDEN
UNDER THE CLOAK OF ANONYMITY OR LOST IN THE MISTS OF
FADING MEMORY—THE AUTHORS KNOWN AS ANON OR TRAD.

# Index of First Lines

# Index

# Index

## Index of Titles